HEADS YOU LOSE
A CLASSIC FROM
CHRISTIANNA BRAND

Bantam offers the finest in classic and modern British murder mysteries.
Ask your bookseller for the books you have missed.

Agatha Christie
Death on the Nile
A Holiday for Murder
The Mousetrap and Other
   Plays
The Mysterious Affair at
   Styles
Poirot Investigates
Postern of Fate
The Secret Adversary
The Seven Dials Mystery
Sleeping Murder

Margery Allingham
Black Plumes
Death of a Ghost
The Fashion in Shrouds

Dorothy Simpson
Last Seen Alive
The Night She Died
Puppet for a Corpse
Six Feet Under
Close Her Eyes

Sheila Radley
The Chief Inspector's
   Daughter
Death in the Morning
Fate Worse than Death

Elizabeth George
A Great Deliverance

John Greenwood
The Missing Mr. Mosley
Mosley by Moonlight
Murder, Mr. Mosley
Mists over Mosley
Coming Soon: The Mind
   of Mr. Mosley

Ruth Rendell
The Face of Trespass
The Lake of Darkness
No More Dying Then
One Across, Two Down
Shake Hands Forever
A Sleeping Life
A Dark-Adapted Eye
   (writing as Barbara
   Vine)
A Fatal Inversion
   (writing as Barbara
   Vine)

Marian Babson
Death in Fashion
Reel Murder

Christianna Brand
Suddenly at His
   Residence
Heads You Lose

Dorothy Cannell
The Widows Club

HEADS YOU LOSE

CHRISTIANNA BRAND

BANTAM BOOKS
TORONTO • NEW YORK • LONDON • SYDNEY • AUCKLAND

*This edition contains the complete text
of the original hardcover edition.*
NOT ONE WORD HAS BEEN OMITTED.

HEADS YOU LOSE

*A Bantam Book / published by arrangement with
the author*

PRINTING HISTORY
First published in 1941
Bantam edition / July 1988

ISBN 0-553-27220-9

Published simultaneously in the United States and Canada

---

*Bantam Books are published by Bantam Books, a division of
Bantam Doubleday Dell Publishing Group, Inc. Its trademark, consisting of the words "Bantam Books" and the por-
trayal of a rooster, is Registered in U.S. Patent and
Trademark Office and in other countries. Marca Registrada.
Bantam Books, 666 Fifth Avenue, New York, New York
10103.*

PRINTED IN THE UNITED STATES OF AMERICA

O   0 9 8 7 6 5 4 3 2 1

*To Dumptsi, my dachsund;
and to Mr. and Mrs. Rhys Rees of Ystalyfera,
for all their kindness to him*

THE CHARACTERS

PENDOCK, the Squire of the Village, and his guests

LADY HART
FRANCESCA HART   } her granddaughters
VENETIA GOLD

HENRY GOLD, Venetia's husband
JAMES NICHOLL
BUNSEN, the butler
GRACE MORLAND, a foolish woman
PIPPI LE MAY, her cousin
TROTTY, their maid

> Among these ten very ordinary
> people were found two
> victims and a murderer.

CHAPTER 1

Grace Morland was sitting on the terrace outside Stephen Pendock's house, putting the finishing touches to a wishy-washy sketch of the Old Church Tower in the Snow. To the left, the railway line made an interesting pattern, smudged abruptly across the plump white downs; to the right a factory chimney reared its sooty finger and a column of grey-black smoke rolled grandly against the wintry sky; but Grace Morland's eye was systematically blinkered against atrocities made by man. She ignored the chimney, put in the downs without the railway, and concentrated upon the church tower which, having been erected to the glory of God, could be relied upon to be picturesque.

It had other advantages than this, for it necessitated a fluttering request that she might be permitted to sit, as quiet as a mouse, upon Stephen Pendock's terrace so as to get the only perfect view. "I shan't be in anybody's way," she had promised, looking up at him with her yearning pale-blue eyes; "I shall sit as quiet as a teeny mouse, and be no trouble to anyone . . ."

It was certainly unlikely that she would be very much in anybody's way, out on a snow-covered terrace in the teeth of a biting wind. "Why, certainly," Pendock had said, eyeing her with tolerant indifference; "as long as you like. But haven't you done it before?"

Of course she had done it before. The Old Church Tower in Bluebell Time, hung, even now, over her mantelpiece at Pigeonsford Cottage; the Church Tower, Autumn, was pushed away into the cupboard underneath Pendock's own stairs, to be produced whenever he had notice of her coming to the house and hung up on the

1

dining-room wall. Spring, summer, autumn and winter she asked, twittering, if she might sit on the terrace and be no trouble to anyone; and spring, summer, autumn and winter she sat so late that he was obliged to ask her to tea or dinner before she went home, and, finally, whether he might not see her to her door; but spring, summer, autumn or winter, so far, he had never proposed.

Pendock was fifty: a tall, straight, good-looking man, with hair growing becomingly grey above his ears, and eyes of a quite amazing deep blue-green. Lying at the edge of a cliff looking down into the clear, cold water of the Cornish seas, you looked into the very depth and colour of Pendock's eyes. Kind eyes, good eyes, humorous, warm, friendly eyes; but not loving eyes; not sentimental eyes; not, anyway, for Grace.

She looked anxiously at her watch. Half-past four and the light was getting so dim that, really, she had no excuse for sitting out there any longer. She pondered the advisability of putting in a plea to be permitted to come again to-morrow; but to-morrow the remains of the snow would probably be gone. It was thick on the downs still, but down here in the valley it was rapidly melting away, and she had had to use a good deal of imagination, even as things were. Of course the *wind* was very cold—it might snow to-night. . . . But surely someone would come out of the house soon, and ask her to stay to tea. Perhaps they had forgotten her. Pendock had guests, she knew: Lady Hart, who had been a friend of his family from the days before he was born, who had stayed at Pigeonsford since his grandfather's time, was there now with her two granddaughters; and Henry Gold who had married Venetia Hart, one of the granddaughters; she imagined them all sitting indoors over a cosy tea—herself, forgotten, left out on the terrace in the bitter cold. There was no pretext for going back into the house, for if she were to keep to her promise of being no trouble to anyone, all she had to do was to walk down the steps of the terrace, pick her way through the melting snow on the lawn, nip over the little bridge that divided Pendock's garden from the orchards that surrounded the Cottage, and be having tea in her own drawing-room by a quarter to five. She began reluctantly to clean up her palette and put her brushes away.

Voices from the french window behind her considerably accelerated this process, and a sleek black dachshund arrived upon the scene and commenced investigations. Venetia Gold and her sister Francesca stepped out on to the terrace.

Miss Morland who had been expecting them for the past half-hour was, of course, quite overcome by surprise. "Oh, Mrs. Gold! Miss Hart! how you startled me! I was just going to pack up my things and creep away quietly to my little house. A teeny mouse, no trouble to anyone!"

"Wouldn't you like some tea before you go?" asked Venetia, politely speaking her piece. "Mr. Pendock said we must bring you in to tea."

"Can we have a look at your picture first?" said Fran, who had rather forgotten what Miss Morland's pictures were apt to be like. "Everything looks so lovely in the snow, doesn't it? Even these rather sloppy downs take on a bit more meaning with the trees so black and the railway line running up the valley and all that. . . ." They both moved round and stood before the easel.

"How exquisite they are!" thought Grace wistfully, for though Venetia was safely married to that dreadful little Jew, Henry Gold, Francesca was only too free, only *too* free, thought Grace darkly, and so very, so painfully, pretty. Venetia was like her name, all Gold: a golden cobweb that looked as if it might, at any moment, to be blown away by the lightest breath of wind to some enchanted land where it really belonged; but Fran, as slim and tall and delicately built as her twin, with the same little hands and narrow, high-arching feet, had yet a look of staunchness about her, a look of courage and resolution as though she would match herself against the world and come out, lightheartedly, the victor. She was as dark as her sister was fair, with black, soft, curling hair and bright, dark eyes; with a generous mouth, generously smeared with scarlet lipstick, so that she looked like a tropical flower blooming in this English garden. Flowers! thought Grace. Cobwebs! If Grace were like a flower, it was a thoroughly British one, a bluebell that looked all right in a wood, but faded and drooped when you came up to it; if she were like a cobweb, it was just an ordinary, dusty grey cobweb, with never a glint of gold. And what chance had she against all this riot of colour and beauty, all this youth and life and gaiety that the Hart sisters carried with them in their shining eyes and eager, exquisite hands; what chance, at thirty-eight, what chance had Grace?

They stood before the picture, hugging their arms because they were cold. "Aziz darling, *not* on Miss Morland's easel," they said to the dachshund; and Venetia, always polite and kind, turned back to the painting and added: "It's awfully pretty, Miss Morland. The church tower. How—how pretty!"

There was a sort of ruthlessness about Fran. She faced the truth so squarely for herself that she could not be hypocritical for others, even to be kind. She struggled to say something nice about the water-colour, but round the edges of her goodwill the truth came bursting forth; she said abruptly: "But why do the church tower, when it's so particularly hideous?"

Poor thing! Just unable to appreciate beauty, that was all. Useless, Grace knew, to try to explain to those that could not see for themselves, the artistic values of a church tower peeping through an orchard, with the little round copse on the right and her own snug cottage pairing off so nicely on the left. Just the roofs visible above Mr. Pendock's fruit trees, no troublesome perspectives at all. . . .

"And besides," said Francesca, peering at the sketch in the gathering dusk, "isn't that the wood where the kitchen-maid was killed?"

A kitchen-maid—not Grace's kitchen-maid or Pendock's, but just a kitchen-maid—had parted with her lover one evening in the previous summer and had subsequently been found in a truly appalling condition: for her hands had been bound behind her with her own belt, and her head severed from her body with one sweep of a large, sharp scythe which lay by her side; and body, head and weapon had been thrown carelessly at the foot of a tree as though the murderer had suddenly grown tired of his ghastly work and abandoned it without care or concealment. It was this very lack of precaution that had made it so hard for the police to find anything to go upon; there was no grim parcel done up in laundry-marked clothes, no surgical dismemberment, no tell-tale length of rope, no sailors' knots. The lover had, of course, been sought out and questioned exhaustively, and friends and relatives had been interviewed again and again, but to no avail. Such few poor shillings as the kitchen-maid had possessed, had remained untouched in her handbag; a tawdry brooch had been torn from her frock, examined perhaps and found to be worthless, and tossed back again on to her breast; beyond this, beyond the pitiful body at the foot of the tree, there had been no sign of what had passed during that night of horror in the little wood. Maniac, avenger, thief?—her assailant had gone his way and left no trace.

Fran led them back through the french windows, into the drawing-room. "Come on, Aziz darling. Oh, look, sweetie, you've got your feet all wet and mucky!" She hoicked the squirming dog into her arms and dried his paws with her handkerchief. "Here's Miss Morland," she announced to Pendock, who stood with his back to the big log fire. "She's been doing the most gruesome picture of the wood where the kitchen-maid was found."

Pendock shuddered, for he had been among the first to be called when a terrified local had stumbled over the girl's body in the copse. "Poor child," he said. "It was a ghastly business; I shall never forget her parents, what a state they were in, and the wretched young man . . . and her—her head. . . ." He went very white and added, as though to turn his thoughts away from the dreadful vision: "It's past clearing up now, I suppose. Some tramp; hoped she might have money. . . ."

"What an upheaval there was in the village," said Fran, tenderly depositing Aziz upon one of the drawing-room chairs. "Detectives and photographers and reporters swarming all over the place. I shouldn't think there's ever been such an excitement here before."

"I hope there never will be again," said Pendock devoutly.

"Were you staying here at the time, then?" asked Grace of Francesca, making ineffectual little dabs at Aziz, who had immediately jumped off the chair and now sat staring disconcertingly into her face.

"It was just at the end of our holiday," explained Venetia. "Fran and Granny were staying with Mr. Pendock as usual, and Henry and I were here for the last week of our honeymoon. It wouldn't have seemed like summer, if I hadn't spent at least part of it with Pen." She smiled at him affectionately.

"And how is dear Lady Hart?"

"Oh, she's all right; she'll be down in a minute. Did you know James Nicholl was here?"

James Nicholl was a young man who kept a sailing-boat in the bay, and spent most of his holidays at the local pub. She remembered him best as a vague, rather droopy, very untidy undergraduate; latterly he had taken a somewhat indifferent interest in his family business and become a little less untidy, though remaining as dreamy as ever. He was under the guardianship of his uncle, a stern old man who had kept a careful eye upon his nephew's more or less blameless activities, until the first threat of war had sent him scuttling off to America; and much good that had done him, thought Grace with self-satisfied irony, for only yesterday she had seen his obituary notices in the papers. No doubt Mr. Nicholl would come in for a nice fat fortune; and she had heard that he was in the Army too . . .

"What a pleasure; and I hear he is in uniform now?"

"Yes, definitely our Brave Boy in Brown," said Fran, gently mocking. "He doesn't know which hand to salute with or who to salute, and I'm sure he's always stepping off with the wrong foot, but otherwise he's tremendous. Mr. Pendock's doing his bit by having him here for his seven days' leave; aren't you, Pen darling?"

Thank goodness for that, anyway, thought Grace, toasting her frozen feet at the fire. Perhaps Francesca would turn her attentions to young Nicholl, now that he had come in for a bit of money, and leave Mr. Pendock alone. Pen darling, indeed! She wished that tea would arrive.

"Here's Granny," said Fran, and the two girls went to the door. "Hallo, darling; have you had your snooze?"

Their grandmother was an old lady whose tiny head looked like nothing so much as a pea perched upon a goodly cottage loaf. She rolled joyously into the room, beaming at them all. ". . . and here's Miss Morland," said Venetia.

"She's been painting the copse where that girl was killed last summer," said Fran, who could not get over this singular choice on the part of the soulful Grace.

Lady Hart looked mildly surprised, but under cover of Grace's protestations sank into a chair. "Thank goodness, here are Henry and James," she said. "I want my tea."

At first glance you would have said that they were an oddly assorted couple to be such close friends. Henry Gold was, without having the characteristic features, unmistakably Jewish. He was a small, slim, ugly man, with a friendly, rather puck-like smile that lit up his face into eagerness and gave him a quite overwhelming charm. James Nicholl, standing in the doorway beside him, was nearly a head taller, with stooping shoulders and heavy-lidded, sleepy eyes, and the rather vacant look of the intellectual mind withdrawn from the teeming personal life without. Henry, beneath a veneer of super-sophistication, was vividly and immediately interested in even the simplest things that made up life; James accorded to time on the wing only the courtesy of a sleepy, mocking, self-deprecatory smile. He alone of the three men was in uniform.

Grace Morland was thrilled. "How splendid to see you, Mr. Nicholl, and in khaki! Or should one say Captain?—or Major? All those lovely pips! I feel quite honoured to shake hands with you."

"Do you?" said James, surprised.

"And were you in France during all that dreadful time? Dunkirk? Do tell me about your adventures. Or perhaps . . ." she lowered her voice to a sickening whisper—"perhaps you'd rather not speak of it?"

James was perfectly willing to speak of it, but not to Miss Morland. "He spent the entire time crouching under a pier," said Henry, to rescue him, "reading a pocket edition of 'Love's Labour's Lost.'"

Jealous, of course. These Jews! "I see that *you're* not in uniform, Mr. Gold," said Grace.

"Henry happens to be in a reserved occupation," said Venetia, flaming at once in defence of her husband. "He offered himself at the very beginning of the war, but they made him stick where he is."

Henry grinned behind his hand. Dear Venetia! As if he cared two hoots what this ridiculous old spinster thought of him; but deep down in his heart his casual dislike took on a sharper form.

Aziz removed himself, apparently in disgust, and embarked upon a complicated toilet in the middle of the hearthrug. "Darling, not here," said Fran, upsetting his equilibrium with the toe of her shoe. "It's rude."

Quite extraordinary, thought Grace, who had been lost in contemplation of a distant object, drawing attention to it like that. She said, for want of something to fill up the gap, which nobody had noticed but herself: "Aziz! what an odd name!"

"It's because he's our Black Boy," said Venetia, as if that explained everything.

Miss Morland looked blank. "After the little doctor, in 'Passage to India,'" explained Henry courteously. "His mother was called Esmiss Esmoor."

Grace assumed her Boots's Library look, tapping her front teeth with her thumb-nail, rolling her faded blue eyes. "'Passage to India—Passage to India.' No! Haven't come across it." That dismissed 'Passage to

India'; but she added affectedly: "Odd; because I'm so fond of travel books."

There was a rather appalling silence; she could see that she had gone wrong somewhere, and sought to cover it by saying brightly: "Fancy having a *dachs*-hund! I don't think I should care to; not in war-time, anyway."

"Wouldn't you? How silly!" said Fran. Lady Hart suggested mildly from her arm-chair that they could hardly put Aziz into cold storage until the war was over.

"Oh, of course I know that some people get very *fond* of a dog," said Grace hastily. "I'm sure he's a dear little fellow. Where did you get him from?"

"He came down by parachute," said James. He added sweetly: "Disguised as a Church of England clergyman." Miss Morland's father had been Rector of Pigeonsford.

"Hence the dog-collar," said Henry. They all went off into fits of slightly hysterical laughter.

An ancient butler arrived with a loaded tray, walking as daintily as a cat upon his corn-tormented feet. "And a parcel has arrived for Miss Fran, Miss. The carrier brought it from the post office at Torrington. It's on the table in the hall."

"It's my new hat," cried Fran, leaping to her feet and clutching him by the arm. "Is it a hatbox, Bunsen? This size, and square?"

"About that size, Miss."

"It is! How lovely! I asked them to send it down, but I never thought it would arrive so soon . . . not that I could wear it here, it would shake the village to its core. You wait, Granny! you're always complaining that our hats nowadays aren't as ridiculous as yours were in the year dot. Well, this one is."

It certainly was. She came back with it perched on her little dark head, smiling and nodding, turning round and round to let them admire its wonders, blushing a little at the look in James's sleepy brown eyes. Pendock felt his heart turn over in a sickening roll as he watched her, so sweet and gay and unaffected, with the absurd little bunch of flowers and feathers perched on her silky head. "Do you like it, Pen?" she said, coming up to him, smiling innocently into his eyes.

Before he could stop himself he had caught her by the hand and pulled her towards him and kissed her, there in front of them all. "You lovely little thing!" he said; and then, conscious of what he had done, he laughed and added lightly: "I think it's a delirious little hat. Don't you, Miss Morland? Don't you think it's a quite remarkable hat?"

Grace sat frozen in her chair, colder than she had been on the terrace outside, in spite of the roaring fire, and knew that this was the failure of all her dreams. She, too, lost control, but not for love of Fran, and cried out spitefully: "Do you call that a hat? I don't call it a hat at all. Good heavens, I wouldn't be seen dead in a ditch in a thing like that!"

They all looked mildly astonished. "I'm sorry you don't like it," said Fran, slowly taking it off. "Of course it's only a bit of nonsense, but I thought it was rather sweet." She supposed Miss Morland was annoyed because she had laughed about her picture.

Grace got up to go. "I didn't mean to be quite so— severe," she said hastily, a little abashed at the sight of Fran's crestfallen face. "I'm sure it's a charming hat, but it's a little more *advanced* than we are quite used to here. I'm afraid in a village, and especially in *war*-time, one gets into the way of thinking perhaps rather too much of the more serious things of life; isn't that so, Mr. Pendock? You who live amongst us can appreciate that; these bright young people from Town. . . ." She thought of London always with a capital letter, as Town.

Pendock was hardly to be expected to enter into a discussion of his guests before their very faces. "You must let me walk across the garden with you," he said. He could not help adding maliciously: "Just to see that you get safely past the copse."

Fran and Venetia came out on to the terrace to see them off. "What a poisonous woman," said Fran, still a little troubled, watching their progress across the snow-sprinkled lawn. "I never did her any harm that I know of; why should she be so loathsome about my hat?"

"I'm afraid it was Pen, not the hat," said Venetia reluctantly. "It looks very much as though he's fallen for you, Fran."

Fran made a little face. "I'm afraid it does. How funny, after all this time."

"It's been coming on for years, Fran, almost since you were a little girl. He always loved you best, though I don't mean to say that he doesn't love me—because, of course, I know he does. But with you it's always been different, and now it's come to a head. I suppose you couldn't fall in love with him, could you? He's so sweet."

Francesca looked doubtful. "Well, I don't know. I do adore him, of *course,* and I should be most divinely rich and live at Pigeonsford for ever . . ."

"You're fairly rich as it is," said Venetia, laughing.

"Yes, I know. That's what makes it so awkward. I mean it cuts out an added incentive, and I don't know whether I love Pen enough to marry him without an added incentive, like terrific wealth or having to be made an honest woman of, or something of that sort. Besides, he's a bit old, *is*n't he?"

"I suppose he is, a bit. But it seems a shame to have two such nice people in love with you as Pen and James, and not to be able to be in love with either of them."

"Well, we don't know about James; he's never actually said anything. I think he only remembers in the intervals of reading Horace and Shakespeare. All the same, I do think it's there."

"Oh, it's there all right, as you call it," said Venetia, smiling. "I only wish that Henry would ever look at me the way James, just occasionally, looks at you."

"Henry adores you," protested Fran.

"Yes, but not in the same way as I adore him, darling; and not in the way James adores you. I suppose you wouldn't understand, not having been in love yourself but only having had people in love with you, how dreadful it is to sort of ache with love for anybody who just comfortably loves you back. Before I was married, such a lot of people ached about me; it was just my luck to pick on the one that only loved me coolly and kindly and affectionately. . . . People all thought Henry was terribly lucky to marry me, I know they did, just because he was a Jew and not very good-looking and not as up in society as some of the others . . . but if they only knew, it was me that was the lucky one; because I wanted Henry so terribly much more than he wanted me. And after six months of marriage, things haven't changed very much. If I were you, Fran, I should marry Pen or James; don't wait for someone you're violently in love with yourself. I assure you it's far more comfortable to be loved than to be in love."

Fran scratched her head, Laurel-fashion, and repeated her little grimace. "Well, I suppose it'll work itself out; anyway, I'd better wait till I'm asked! It's funny, though, when you think that we used to look upon Pen as an uncle, when we were little girls."

"Not so funny for Pen," said Venetia seriously.

Pendock did not think so either. Walking across the lawn at Miss Morland's side, he was deep in thought, cursing those crinkly grey hairs on either side of his handsome head. "Fran must be twenty-four or five," he thought, "and I'm exactly twice her age. Why does she get lovelier every time she comes to Pigeonsford? She used to be a little leggy dark-haired colt of a creature, and goodness knows I thought I loved her then; but now she's a woman, for all her childishness. . . . I can't keep it back any longer. I shall have to speak to Lady Hart. . . ."

He became conscious that his companion was talking, talking rapidly and rather hysterically, pouring forth the flood of her angry jealousy: ". . . so, really, Mr. Pendock, you must forgive me for being so abrupt with one of your guests, but to see her posturing and preening herself in that dreadful little hat and with all that paint on her face, well, really, when I was her age—and no doubt that's a very long time ago—I was taught to believe that only women of loose morals behaved like that. Of course we poor village people can't be expected to keep up with all the smart London set and their ways, but really—well, now, honestly, in your heart, Mr. Pendock, what would you think of *me* if *I* were to behave in such a way?"

The thought of Grace Morland moving among them as Francesca had done, laughing and blushing and showing off that dear little, funny little hat, was so grotesque that Pendock could only laugh. He did not know that she was jealous, only that she was absurd. He stood with his hand on the gatepost, looking at her and laughing, and all his heart was warm with the thought of Fran. Grace, listening to his laughter, shivering from the tender, far-away look in his eyes, screamed at him suddenly, all her defences down: "You would say that I was what *she* is; you would say that I was no better than a—no better than a—nothing but a *tart*!"

She burst open the door of her house and ran, weeping, up to her room.

Fran, first of the women to come down to dinner that evening, paused for a moment at the door of the drawing-room. James Nicholl stood with his back to the tall Adam mantelpiece, a cocktail-glass in his hand, looking as usual more than half asleep. He roused himself sufficiently to say as she came across the room towards him: "You look like an orchid, Fran; one of those big Catelyas. I don't know how you contrive to be so full of colour when you're wearing a plain grey dress."

James made her nervous, lately. She did not know whether or not to take him seriously, and now she said lightly: "Thank you, my pet. It's not often we hear such pretty speeches from you."

"You're going to hear a very pretty one indeed, if only the rest of the party will take a bit longer to dress," he said, still not hurrying his words. "I observed for the first time, to-day, that our Pen has got his eye on you; and in case you should make up your mind too quickly in his favour, I thought I'd better so far abuse his hospitality as to inform you that I also am in the running. I don't know if you knew. Have a cocktail?"

She looked at him, bewildered, but accepted the cocktail. "I feel I need it. Is this a proposal, James?"

"It would be, if there was time," said James, glancing towards the door. "But it's rather a long story. Do you think you could bear to listen to it some time this evening?"

"Well, James, of *course*. I mean, I don't mean 'of course' to the proposal, but of course I'd like to listen to the story and—and then—well, we could—see. But we can't very well march off by ourselves after dinner, if that's what you mean."

"You think Pendock might not be too pleased? No, you're right, I don't think he would. On the other hand, I've made up a beautiful speech and I'd like you to hear it. Look here; will you meet me after they've all pushed off to bed? Come out on the terrace—or, better still, come down to the orchard and we'll go for a walk in the moonlight. It's a lovely evening for courting."

Pendock came in, followed after a few minutes by Lady Hart. "Sherry for me, please, Pen dear. Fran, what's the matter? You look rather white."

"I can't possibly, darling; I've got pots of rouge on. Where's the Black Boy?"

Venetia and Henry arrived, and Aziz came busily in at the heels of the butler. "Come on, my enemy alien," said Fran, picking him up in her arms. "What an old faggot that Morland is! Fancy saying she wouldn't have him, just because he's a mouldy German . . . my heavenly one. . . ." She trailed off into the dining-room, murmuring lovingly into a velvet ear.

They sat down to dinner: Pendock at one end of the glowing old mahogany table, Lady Hart on his right, jolly and vivacious in her flowing black velvet frock, a scrap of old lace sitting crookedly on top of her head to hide the scarcity of her soft white hair; Venetia on his left, her hair a shining halo round her little head; Fran, rather silent, still a trifle white under the pots of rouge.

Henry contributed a theory that Aziz had been a simple British bull-dog doing a spot of secret service work in Germany, when suddenly the wind had changed. . . .

Bunsen came in with the coffee. "And a telephone call for Captain Nicholl, sir."

"For me?" said James, surprised. "Who on earth knows I'm here?" He rose to his feet. "Well, I'd better go and find out, I suppose. Don't say they're packing up my leave!"

It was a very long call. They drank their coffee and poured out glasses of port. James came back, looking a little strained. "It was nothing. Just somebody—ringing me up."

"*No!*" said Venetia, laughing.

They moved off into the drawing-room, and settled down to Vingt-et-un. "I don't think I'll play," said James, counting out matches with a casual forefinger. "I've got a bit of a headache. I'll go for a stroll outside." Over their unsuspecting heads he signalled to Francesca: "The orchard—eleven o'clock."

So that at half-past ten Fran yawned prodigiously and announced that it was terribly late, and she thought they all ought to go to bed. As her present passion for Vingt-et-un usually kept them up till the early hours of the morning, this declaration was received with astonishment, not unmingled with relief. Aziz departed for a brief and business-like walk upon the terrace and a second handkerchief was sacrificed to his muddy paws; he went contentedly upstairs, tucked under Venetia's arm. Pendock, key in hand, stood at the front door and called out: "Is James in?"

Fran applied her ear to the door of James's room. "He says he's gone to bed," she called back, hanging over the banisters; "he's still got a headache and he wants to go to sleep."

Pendock locked the door and came slowly upstairs. "I hope we're not getting flu or anything," he said. "I feel rather rotten myself. Ought I to go in and see if he's all right?"

"No, no, he's fine," said Fran hastily. "You know what it is when you've got a headache; he just wants to be left alone." She made a private resolution to be terribly nice to Pen to-morrow to make up for all these lies.

"Don't you want to say good-night to Aziz, Pen?" Venetia was saying, obligingly thrusting a black face up to his. "Kiss your Uncle Pen good-night, angel. There! Isn't he sweet?"

"*Don't* let him lick people, darling."

"Now, Granny, you're getting like the Morland. Pen likes saying good-night to him, don't you, Pen?"

"Couldn't sleep without it," said Pen, laughing, retreating to his room. "Good-night, Venetia; good-night, Lady Hart; good-night, Fran."

"Good-night, Aziz," said Fran, laying her cheek against the soft tan muzzle. "Sleep tight, my sweetie; don't forget, Venetia, it's my turn to have him to-morrow. Good-night, darling. Good-night, Henry. Good-night, Gran. . . ."

She slipped into her room and stood behind the door.

CHAPTER 2

Pendock was dreaming. He dreamt that he was walking down a long, dim tunnel and that at the end of the tunnel, out in the light, stood the figure of a woman. It seemed to him of terrible importance that he should see the woman's face. He struggled towards her, dragging his leaden limbs, and, coming out into the sunshine, put his hand under her chin; but just as he was about to lift her face, there was a tremendous thundering in the tunnel behind him. He turned to see what was making the noise, and when he turned back again, the woman was gone . . . and he was lying in bed with the strangest sense of foreboding in his head and heart. There was a loud, insistent knocking at his door.

"Come in!" he called, sitting up and switching on his bedside lamp; something must be wrong, for it was not yet midnight.

Lady Hart came into the room and towards the bed; she was clad in a dressing-gown, and her kind old face was shockingly white and drawn. She said, before he could speak: "Pen, you must come at once. Something dreadful's happened, and I'm . . ." She seemed reluctant to say it but at last she burst out: "I'm terrified!"

"*What's* happened?" he said, struggling into his dressing-gown, pushing his feet into slippers.

"Bunsen has found a girl—has seen a girl——" She was trembling all over and she leant for a moment against the bedpost. "There's a woman lying in the garden, Pen, down by the drive. She—I—she seems to be wearing Fran's hat—Fran's new little hat. . . ."

"But Fran—where's Fran?" he said sharply, his heart like ice.

17

"She's not in her room," said Lady Hart, swaying, clinging to the bedpost now. "Her—her bed hasn't been slept in. I went straight there. Pen—she's not in her room. . . ." She slid gently into a faint and lay in a huddled heap on the floor beside the bed.

Pendock did not even see her. He was taking the stairs three at a time, wrestling with the lock of the big front door, leaping the steps and running out into the moonlit garden, sick with a horrible dread. Bunsen came across the lawn to meet him, white-faced, with protruding eyes. "This way, sir; down by the gate. My god, sir, it's dreadful; she's—her head . . ."

She was lying in a ditch that ran by the side of the drive and down to the little stream; he could see her quite clearly in the moonlight, her legs at a dreadful angle, her arms bent under her, her head—her head had been hacked from her body and then clapped back again on to her neck; and on top of this dreadful, this bloodless, lolling head was thrust, in all its absurdity, Fran's new hat. A mist like blood passed before his eyes; he closed them to shut out the horror of it, and falling at last on to his sagging knees, he started to crawl towards the horrible figure, going up close to it, flinging aside that frightful, that obscene gay hat; and pushing away the dark hair that hung, blood-clotted, across the face, he staggered to his feet and, at the side of the ditch, lay panting and vomiting till the world was still again.

But it was not Francesca's lovely face that had leered out at him, dark and distorted, from the tangle of dripping hair; the body in the ditch, the severed head, the face beneath the brave little hat—they were Grace Morland's.

Lady Hart had roused herself by the time Pendock got back to the house, and was sitting on the edge of his bed, still looking frightened and dazed. "It's Grace Morland," he said, wasting no time. "She's been murdered. We've got to get hold of Fran."

She looked as though she would faint again, but pulled herself together and staggered to her feet.

"Thank God it isn't Fran—I was terrified. I couldn't think straight. . . . I'm afraid I must have fainted after I spoke to you, and I've just been sitting here, trying to pull myself together. We'd better go to her room."

She was curled up like a kitten, apparently sound asleep in her bed. As they switched on the light, she stirred and turned over and opened a drowsy eye. "Who is it? What is it? Granny! Is it an air raid?"

Lady Hart stared at her, thunderstruck. "Francesca! How long have you been in bed?"

"How long?" asked Fran, pushing back her hair and sitting up staring at them. "All night; well, I mean, ever since I came to bed. I've been asleep for hours."

"There's been an accident," said Pendock, coming forward into the room. "Something's happened to Grace Morland. They've found her—well, she's dead, poor thing."

"*Dead?* Grace Morland? How could she be dead?"

Terror had made Pendock angry and irritable. He said roughly: "By the simple expedient of having her head cut off."

The door of Venetia's room opened and she came out in her dressing-gown, the dachshund clasped in her arms. "I thought I heard voices. Has something happened? Is it an air raid?"

"Grace Morland's had her head cut off," said Fran, and burst into hysterical laughter.

Lady Hart looked warningly at Pendock and sat down on the edge of the bed, her arm round her grand-daughter's shoulders. "Hush, darling. Calm yourself. You're behaving badly. I'm afraid poor Miss Morland's had an accident, Venetia. They found her in the garden. Pen's just been down to see."

Henry Gold appeared, moving quietly into their midst, dark and a little mysterious, his quick eyes searching their faces. Venetia ran to him. "Henry, Grace Morland's been killed!"

"Grace Morland?" he said. "What, the woman who was here this afternoon? How on earth could she have got killed?"

"She's been murdered," said Pendock harshly, maddened by their stupidly staring eyes and bewildered speech. "It's the same as the girl in the summer. She's lying in the culvert at the bottom of the drive, and she's had her head cut off. Bunsen is there, and I got hold of one of the gardeners."

"Have you rung up the police?" said Henry.

"No, I haven't had time to think. I suppose we'd better do that at once. And does one get a doctor?"

"Not if you're sure she's dead. The police will see to it."

"She's dead all right," said Pendock savagely, seeing again that dreadful corpse in the ditch. "Her head— look here, Henry, go and ring the police for me, will you? I've had a bit of a shock and I feel rather . . . ghastly. . . ." He walked like an automaton into his bedroom and closed the door.

Pigeonsford village is a collection of cottages and small shops that have grown up around what is commonly known as the "'Ouse." Its single constable could by no means be got to understand that Miss Morland had been murdered and her body left in Mr. Pendock's drive. Henry Gold contented himself with instructions that the constable should come round immediately, and himself rang up the station at Torrington fifteen miles away. Inspector Cockrill replied without excitement that he would be over in half an hour.

Fran meanwhile had insisted upon waking James. She leant over his bed, shaking him out of a deep and tuneful sleep. "James, do wake up. Do wake up."

"Wassamarrer?" said James, heaving the bed-clothes back over his shoulders.

"James, come on, wake up. Something dreadful's happened. *Do* wake up!"

Lady Hart went to the wash-basin and liberally wetted a sponge. "Try this; I never knew it to fail."

Fran mercifully wrung out some of the water, and applied the sponge gingerly to James's face. He sprang upright and sat blinking at them from under his tousled hair. "Here, what's going on? What the hell are you doing?"

"If you say 'Is it an air raid?' I shall scream," said Lady Hart.

"Something dreadful's happened," said Fran again. "Miss Morland's been killed, out in the garden."

"Grace Morland?" said James, dumbfounded.

"Yes, she's been killed, poor thing, and the police will be here asking us a lot of questions, and they'll want to know whether we've all been in bed all night and things like that; of course we have, but we thought we'd better wake you up and tell you what was happening. . . ."

A very faint grin appeared upon James's face.

They were sitting in solemn conclave when Henry came back. "Well, I've rung up the police; I had a frightful time getting hold of anyone with sense, but I finally asked for Cockie and he's coming over right away." He stood before them, excitement struggling with conventional regret. "How was it discovered?"

"It was me," said Lady Hart, shivering. "At least it wasn't me that actually found Miss Morland, of course, but Bunsen, and he told me and I told Pen. I heard a noise, and there was Bunsen out on the terrace, throwing stones at Pen's window, the one next to mine. I asked him what he was doing, and he said that there was a girl, or a woman—he actually said 'a young lady' I believe—lying in the garden, down by the drive, near the gate. He was terribly upset, poor old Bunsen, and panting like anything from running across the lawns to get Pen."

"Why the devil didn't he go straight to Pen's room?"

"The front door would be locked and it's miles round by the back; it was the obvious thing to do—don't interrupt, Henry. Go on, Gran!"

"I said to him, 'Who is the woman?' and he said he didn't know. Her hair was all over her face; but she had on Miss Fran's hat."

"My *hat*?" cried Fran.

"Well, that's what Bunsen said, and he'd seen you with it at tea-time. I expect he was wrong, because what would Miss Morland be doing with your hat? But of course immediately I thought it was you and that's why I—that's why I went and called Pen," finished Lady Hart, rather lamely.

Nobody noticed it. "Oh, Bunsen must be wrong," said Fran, flushed and excited. "It couldn't be my hat. Anyway, it's still on the table in the hall—I can soon find out." She ran to the stairs and looked over the banisters to where the box stood, open and empty, its lid on the chair beside the hall-stand, a trail of tissue paper littering the table. Henry came to her side and looked over also. "I'm afraid it's gone," he said.

Inspector Cockrill was a little brown man who seemed much older than he actually was, with deep-set eyes beneath a fine broad brow, an aquiline nose and a mop of fluffy white hair fringing a magnificent head. He wore his soft felt hat set sideways, as though he would at any moment break out into an amateur rendering of "Napoleon's Farewell to his Troops"; and he was known to Torrington and in all its surrounding villages as Cockie. He was widely advertised as having a heart of gold beneath his irascible exterior; but there were those who said bitterly that the heart was so infinitesimal and you had to dig so deep down to get to it, that it was hardly worth the trouble. The fingers of his right hand were so stained with nicotine as to appear to be tipped with wood.

He looked very much shocked when he saw the poor body lying so crookedly in the ditch at the bottom of Pigeonsford drive. He had known Grace Morland since her girlhood. Her father had united him (after a little speech which had subsequently proved to have been over-optimistic) to his wife; had buried her when, worn out with the struggle of producing one rather underweight child, she had incontinently died; had buried the child when shortly afterwards it too had died, and with it all his hope and much of his faith and charity. Grace had set her cap at him in after years, but half heartedly, for he was not to be considered her equal in breeding or education; he thought of her, without rancour, as a sentimental goat. But what an end for her to have come to, poor creature! And her head—he gingerly took hold of it by the hair. . . .

Lady Hart and the girls were huddled up on sofas in the drawing-room when, in the early hours of the morning, he came wearily up to the house. Venetia had Henry beside her to hold her hand; but Fran, from very excess of would-be comforters, sat by herself, with Aziz asleep in her lap. An agitated maid handed round strong black coffee.

Cockrill accepted a cup. "And perhaps you'd send some down to my men in the garden, Mr. Pendock? Sorry about all this; it's a shock for you." His bright eyes flickered from face to face. He thought: "*One* young lady hasn't been too much shocked to remember to put on her make-up; or else she never took it off. I wonder . . ."

Pendock said diffidently: "What about Miss Morland's house, Inspector? She's got an elderly maid—well, of course you'll know her—old Trotty, and I'm afraid this will be a dreadful thing for her. Have you thought about letting her know?"

Cockrill gave him a quizzical glance. "Oh yes, I've thought about it."

"I'm sorry," said Pendock, flushing. "I don't want to seem officious."

Cockrill smiled at him. "Oh, that's all right. But I'll see to everything; you can safely leave it to me. Now, about this business? Any of you people know anything?"

"My dear Cockie, how could we *poss*ibly?" said Fran; she and Venetia had known him from their childhood.

He looked at her squarely, and then, producing a paper and tobacco, rolled himself an untidy cigarette. "Mr. Pendock, what about your butler? What was he doing coming home at twelve o'clock?"

"He went over to see his sister at Tenfold," said Venetia.

"That's right, Inspector. I gave him permission to go over after dinner. She's been ill, and he had a 'phone call to say that she was worse. He told me, while we were waiting for you, that he found her very bad and had to get hold of Dr. Newsome, from Torrington; he knew I wouldn't mind his getting back late. He's been with me for years and does more or less what he likes."

"And can you confirm that his sister is, in fact, ill at Tenfold?"

Pendock was taken aback. "Good heavens, yes; what are you suggesting? I saw her myself, two or three days ago. Anyway, Newsome'll tell you."

"All right, all right, all right; just asking," said Cockie equably. "So the butler found the poor lady and informed you, Lady Hart; is that right?"

Lady Hart was by now sufficiently recovered to throw a little drama into her account of the awakening by Bunsen. ". . . so I went at once to Mr. Pendock's room and told him what had happened and then, I'm afraid, I collapsed."

"I rushed down to the drive," said Pendock, sitting up on the sofa and handing his cup to the parlour-maid for refilling. "When I found that it was Miss Morland, I left Bunsen with her and got hold of a man to stay with him, and came back to the house, and we roused the others."

"In what order?" said Cockie, carefully avoiding a glance at Fran's make-up.

"Well, actually, Venetia and Mr. Gold woke themselves; first we went to Fran's room . . ."

"Why to hers? Why not, for example, to Captain Nicholl's?"

"Because Francesca's room is opposite Mr. Pendock's, where we were," said Lady Hart quickly. "We went there first, simply because it was nearest. My granddaughter was in bed and asleep." She did not look at Pendock. "After that the others arrived and later on we went and roused James; he was still sound asleep, and we had some trouble in waking him. It was then that we found out that the hat was missing . . ." She broke off suddenly.

"The hat?" said Cockie sharply. "What hat was that?"

"Well, it's a very extraordinary thing, Inspector," said Pendock uneasily. "Fran had a new hat sent to her this afternoon—yesterday afternoon," he corrected, looking at his watch. "Anyway, she left it in a box on the hall table. No doubt you noticed that Miss Morland had a—was wearing a little flowered hat? Well, that was Fran's."

"Not *wearing* it," said Cockie, thinking back. "She didn't have it on her head when I saw her."

"*Did*n't she? I'm sure she——" He pressed his forehead against the palm of his hand: "Ah, yes, of course, I must have taken it off. . . . I believe now that I flung it aside so that I could see the face. I was so terrified that it was Fran, there in the ditch; I—I had to see the face."

"Why should you have thought it was Fran?" said Cockie, deeply interested.

"Because of the hat, of course," said Lady Hart sharply.

"Ah, yes. The hat. But, actually, she was fast asleep in bed?"

"Yes," said Pendock and Lady Hart and Fran together.

"And Captain Nicholl was also asleep in bed; and what about Venetia?"

"Well, I was asleep too, Cockie, of course."

"And Mr. Gold? You were sharing Venetia's room?"

"Actually I was sleeping in the dressing-room; but if you're suggesting . . ." began Henry hotly.

"All right, all right; just asking."

He took a brief note of their movements from the time they had last seen Grace Morland and then sent them all off upstairs. "I'm going back to Pigeonsford Cottage now" (Pendock noted the "back"), "but I'll be here first thing in the morning. You won't mind, Mr. Pendock, if I leave a man on guard in the hall?"

"I don't mind, of course," said Pendock. "But why in the hall? There's nothing to guard out there."

"That's just what I want to guard," said Cockie, rising and stretching his weary limbs, clapping his shabby old hat sideways on to his head. "Nothing. It's very interesting—when it's in a cardboard box." He stumped off into the night.

They trailed up the stairs, but they could not go to bed; soon they were collected again, sitting about on the landing, perched on the window-sill or propped against the big oak chest; Fran sat on the top step, Aziz in her arms, gazing down to the hall where a sleepy constable guarded the empty box. The hat. Everything seemed to turn upon the hat. Why should that pitiful corpse have been made ridiculous with Fran's nonsensical little hat? They thought wildly of feuds and vendettas, of strange superstitions and creeds . . . and then with a wild relief of the kitchen-maid in the wood. Of course! A maniac. Not a pretty thought, but at least, ridiculous though it seemed to say such a thing, at least a *sane* one. A maniac had struck again, and this time had satisfied some crazy impulse by decking the body of the victim with the first bit of brightness and colour that came to hand. But to whose hand? Who could have had access to that hat-box on the hall table? Henry said, for the hundredth time: "You're sure the front door was locked?"

"Of course I'm sure," said Pendock irritably. "You all saw me doing it; and I remember struggling with the lock, trying to get out of the door. . . ." Fumbling with the key, battling with the well-known little difficulty in turning it, and all the time with that sickening dread in his heart: half crazy with terror that he might find Fran, his lovely one, lying in the ditch with her beautiful head hacked off . . . of course, of course he was sure!

"What about the french windows?" suggested Fran, leaning back against the banisters, smoking a cigarette; "after all there are french windows to all the downstairs rooms . . . the drawing-room, and the dining-room the other side of the hall, and the library, at the back . . . couldn't one of them have been left open?"

"It doesn't sound like Bunsen, does it?" said Venetia doubtfully.

Bunsen had been with Pendock's father when Pendock himself had been only a boy; the Hart sisters had grown up under his mild blue eyes, and, apart from his sister in Tenfold, these were the only three people in the world he loved. Pendock he treated with a respectful austerity; but Fran and Venetia were the darlings of his heart, and he spent long hours devising small surprises and treats for them, dreaming over their futures and delighting in all their pretty little ways. He was a gentle old man, with a round, pink, wrinkled face and a fringe of neatly brushed silver hair; the impeccability of his dress broke down abruptly at his shoes which were stretched and slashed to accommodate his corns: he wore his trousers very long, in consequence. His whole life had been spent in the service of Pigeonsford, and if there were indeed a great world outside its gates, it was of no interest to him. It was very unlikely indeed that Bunsen had been careless with locks and bolts. "Still we might just *ask* him," said Fran, scrambling to her feet.

He was sitting at the kitchen table when she and Pendock found him, a hot cup of tea before him. He raised to his master weary and haunted eyes.

"Why don't you go and get some sleep, Bunsen?" said Pendock kindly.

The old man stumbled to his feet. "I can't, sir. I keep seeing the poor lady. You was warned, sir, and you took it bad enough; me, I just—just come upon it, lying there by the drive, and I can't get it out of me mind. Not that I knew then that the 'ead was off, Mr. Pendock, sir: I don't think I could ever have got across them lawns if I had. But I thought it was Miss Fran with 'er dark 'air all over her face and that little hat on her head—so help me God, I thought it was our Miss Fran. . . ." He buried his face in his hands, but after a moment he said apologetically: "Begging your pardon, Miss Fran dear, for I shouldn't be saying this in front of you, I know."

"Oh, Bunsen, don't think of it; try to blot it out. And, look, don't drink that tea—it'll only keep you awake."

"You must go to bed, Bunsen, and take some aspirin or something," said Pendock. "Sleep as long as you can; Cook and the girls can see to things in the morning . . . don't you get up. But, I say, Bunsen—before you go: you locked up as usual last night?"

"Oh yes, sir, just as usual; all but the front door and that, of course, I left for you just as I always do."

"And the windows and things? Don't be afraid to say; it would be a relief to know that there had been some way into the house."

"I locked 'em all, sir, before I started for Tenfold," said Bunsen, shocked at the bare suggestion that he might have failed in so important a duty; for was there not talk of an invasion, and a nice thing if he should be capable of leaving doors and windows open at such a time! "And the back door; I had to use my key to it when I got back to the house. If you're doubtful, sir, we can go round and see; but you'll find they're all in order, sir—I'm sure you will."

The constable, who had followed them into the kitchen, was not prepared for a round tour of the house. "The Inspector's seen to it already," he said. "Everything locked all right." He gave a rather dreadful sniff.

"Thank you," said Penfold, but he did not feel very thankful; for if the house had been securely locked all night, how had the maniac got in? And supposing he had got in, what had he originally come for? Not for the hat, for, apart from himself and his guests, nobody knew about that.

Evidently Fran was following the same train of thought, for she said suddenly: "Bunsen: about my hat? You didn't mention it to anybody this evening? To the servants, or to anyone in Tenfold?"

"No indeed, Miss Fran. What would I mention it for?"

"Well, I know it seems silly, Bunsen, but did you? To amuse your sister perhaps. . . ."

"I never said a word about it, Miss," said Bunsen positively. "Not even in the 'all, and I'm perfectly certain of it. I don't know that I might not have done so, if you'll excuse me, Miss, for indeed you did look a picture in that 'at. Miss Fran put it on her head in front of the mirror in the hall, sir," he explained to Pendock, "and, 'What do you think of it, Bunsen?' she says to me, and 'I think it's a treat, Miss,' I says; didn't I, Miss Fran? But when I got back to the kitchen Cook had took a message to say my sister was worse again, and from that moment I didn't think of nothing else but that, and of course of my work. As soon as I'd taken the coffee into the dining-room, I got on my bicycle and went off to Tenfold, and from then on everything else was drove right out of my head."

"Well, all right, Bunsen, off you go to bed. I'm sorry to have worried you; forget about it—it's nothing. Good-night, and don't get up in the morning until you're thoroughly rested. The maids can see to things."

"Good-night, Bunsen dear," said Fran, and put her hand for a moment on the old man's arm. "Sleep tight, and—try not to think about things." She smiled at him and went back with Pen up the stairs.

Most of the rest of the party had gone to bed. Venetia, however, put her head out of her door to say: "I say, Pen, we couldn't have left the french window open when we let Aziz out for his widdle?"

"I shut the damn thing myself," said Pen reluctantly. Fran was looking more and more depressed.

For how awkward, thought Fran, that she and James should have chosen that one night of all nights to go down and talk in the orchard, leaving the back door open so that they could get in again. Not that it could have anything to do with the murder, of course; but she supposed that the maniac might have come in that way for some unexplained purpose and, seeing the hat in its box on the table, have taken it out and carried it off to decorate the poor dead body in the ditch; unless Miss Morland herself . . . but how could she have known the back door would be open just for those few short minutes? Why should she have wanted the hat? She thought it was a dreadful hat; she had said that she wouldn't be seen dead in a ditch in it. . . .

And now she *was* dead. Dead in a ditch, in the hat. And only six people—she faced it squarely, as she faced everything in life—only six people had heard her say those words: herself and Venetia, her twin, her other half; and Granny, who was father and mother and friend to them both; and Pen—dear Pen, best and kindest and most honourable of men; and Henry, whom Venetia so desperately loved; and James. James, who had held her in his arms in the orchard; had held her crushed against him, until her body ached, and poured out such a torrent of love and longing . . . lazy, sleepy James who had suddenly woken up. Venetia and Granny and Pen and Henry and James. Nobody else had heard.

CHAPTER 3

Breakfast next morning was a rather ghastly affair, for most of them had lain awake as Fran had done, putting two and two together, and arriving at somewhat similar conclusions. The meal was punctuated by the sound of noisy feet and the loud cries of Cockie's henchmen, who had taken possession of the house and were subjecting it to a very severe scrutiny. The hall was closed to the family, and they had been obliged to make a series of detours to reach the dining-room. By this route also came a young lady who was introduced, disapprovingly, by Bunsen as: "Miss le May, with Inspector Cockrill's permission, sir."

Miss Pippi le May stood regarding them with inquisitive grey-green eyes. She was a tiny creature with a stringy little body and small, expressive brown hands. Her hair, which Nature had made red and Art had assisted into a handsome auburn, was so thick and close-cut that it made a sort of woolly cap about her head; she had wound a bright scarf around it and joined the ends gaily with a couple of gigantic gold hair-pins; there was an air of chic about her, but all the washing in the world could not make her look quite clean. She was a not unsuccessful character actress making her determined way upon the West End stage. And she was Grace Morland's cousin.

Pendock rose to meet her. "Miss le May! I'd no idea you were down. Or have you just arrived?"

"I arrived last night," said Pippi briefly. She tipped her hand to her head in a casual salute. "Morning, Lady Hart. Hallo, Venetia. Hallo, Fran. Oh, hallo, James."

"Hallo, Pippi," they said, staring at her.

Pendock pulled up a chair to the table. "Thank you," she said, accepting it calmly. "Can I have some coffee? What a mess this is about poor old Grace, isn't it?"

"It's the most ghastly affair," said Pendock, looking at her with troubled eyes.

"She seemed a bit agitato when I got here last night. I thought it was because I'd just turned up, and you know what an old fuss-pot she was, she liked about six weeks' notice; but I'd only decided yesterday, myself, and I was darned if I was going to bust ninepence on a telegram or whatever it is with these ghastly war-time prices."

"You could have 'phoned here; we'd very gladly have taken her a message," and Pen, for Pigeonsford Cottage did not rise to a telephone.

"Oh, a trunk call would have been just as much; and as a matter of fact I never thought about it at all."

"You say she seemed agitated and upset?"

"Well, she looked as if she'd been howling and her nerves were all on edge; this was at about eight o'clock."

"What time did you last see her?" said several voices at once.

"Good heavens, you're as bad as old Cockrill; he arrived at some unearthly hour this morning and hoicked us out of bed and started asking us the most peculiar questions. We finally worked it out that we last saw her just after eleven o'clock, when we went to bed. Trotty gave me some Horlicks and stuff, and went off to give Grace hers. She came back and said that Grace was in a great state of excitement and quite different from what she had been earlier in the evening; she said she was running round and round the room like a chicken with its head cut off. . . . Oh dear," said Pippi, clapping her hand to her mouth and regarding them over it with humorously horrified eyes: "What a very unfortunate metaphor!"

"I should just go on with what you were saying, my dear," said Lady Hart, though she did not regard Pippi as her dear, at all.

"Well, anyway, she was flapping round, saying that now she had somebody in the hollow of her hand, or some such expression."

"Who on earth could she have meant?" said Fran, quite thrilled.

"Goodness knows. Actually her expression was 'a certain person'—a bit vague, and, as reported by Trotty, vaguer still. What's all this about a hat?" asked Pippi abruptly.

They had not mentioned the hat that morning. There had been a sort of reticence about it, as though its significance were too deep, and possibly too dangerous, to be lightly put into words. They stiffened at Pippi's crude question. Pendock said: "Hasn't the Inspector told you?"

"He asked me a devil of a lot of questions which didn't seem to me to make sense at all. How could I be expected to know anything about some hat of Fran's?"

But perhaps she had known, thought Venetia, and the horrors of the night seemed to lift like a dark cloud from about her heart. Here was escape from the ghastly conclusions of the early hours of the morning, when life and humour and a sense of proportion had been at their lowest ebb. Grace might have told Pippi, her cousin; she might have told Trotty, her old maid-servant. Trotty might have told half the village. Perhaps dozens of people had known that Grace Morland had said that she wouldn't be seen dead in the hat; now, in the dear, familiar white-panelled dining-room, with its warmth and beauty, the thin winter sunshine streaming in through the high french windows, she could suddenly see that it might have been all a coincidence. Somehow or other, perhaps to spite Fran, Miss Morland had got hold of the hat; and coming back from the house with it, had been overtaken and murdered and her body thrown into the culvert at the side of the drive. No need for the ghastly, shadowy suspicions that last night she had felt she couldn't tell even Henry about; no need for any of their beloved ones to be involved; all clear, all easy, all simply explicable. She turned eagerly to Pippi le May.

"Didn't Miss Morland mention to you or to Trotty that Fran had this particular hat? Miss Morland didn't like it; she thought it was frivolous and silly, and her last words to Pen at her door were something to that effect. . . . I expect her mind would be full of it and she'd say something to Trotty about it as soon as she got into the house. . . ."

"I can't say, not having been there at the time," said Pippi indifferently. "She certainly didn't mention it to me, and Trotty says she's heard nothing about it. Does it make any difference?"

Lady Hart could see that Fran was distressed by all this talk of the hat. Fran felt it shocking and dreadful that her comic little hat should have been put to so horrible a purpose, as though she were in some way to blame because Grace Morland was dead and made ludicrous, poor silly woman. She said, to change the subject: "Why are you down here, Pippi? I thought you were in a revue?"

"I got a few days off," said Pippi airily. "We've got a new idea—we swap the turns about so that it's never the same on consecutive nights; it's pretty hot, actually, because people come time after time, knowing that they'll see the same artists and some of the same numbers, but always some different ones. The best of it is that it doesn't make much difference if one or other of the cast is away, so it's fairly easy to wangle a day or two off, if it's absolutely necessary."

They could not help reflecting that it could hardly be absolutely necessary for Pippi to wangle a day or two off to pay a visit to her cousin Grace. She spent most of her summer holidays there, as she had done since she had been a schoolgirl; for Pigeonsford village is not very far from the sea, and Grace had a baby car and a month with her cost Pippi nothing. But, in the depth of winter, with nothing more gay than a Village Institute Party in Tenfold or tea at the Vicarage . . .

James Nicholl had known her better than any of them, in the old days, for she had always been very willing to go sailing with him in the *Greensleeves* and to stay and drink beer in the pub when the Pigeonsford party had gone decorously home to dinner; perhaps it was this old familiarity that emboldened him to say suddenly: "Er—Pippi. What were you doing last night between half-past ten and eleven?"

Pippi put down her coffee-cup with a little clonk; but it was the briefest possible moment before she said coolly, "I got bored with Grace and Trotty and went out for a stroll in the orchard; it was nice in the moonlight with the snow on the downs and so forth. I'm afraid, Mr. Pendock, that I may have been trespassing on your property; but it runs so close to the Cottage that I'm always getting mixed up. The orchard's yours actually, isn't it?"

"It's all mine," said Pendock briefly. "I lease the Cottage to Miss Morland."

"Did you see anyone in the orchard?" asked James, apparently not interested in the layout of Mr. Pendock's property.

"I thought I saw a man strolling there too," said Pippi promptly. "It may have been imagination, and I certainly couldn't say who it was; but I thought there was someone there. I had to tell the police, of course."

At half-past ten, thought Lady Hart, they had all been in the drawing-room, playing Vingt-et-un; all, that was, except James, who had said that he had a headache and would go for a stroll outside. But by eleven o'clock he had come in and gone straight to his room. Fran had said so; she had leaned over the banisters and called down to Pen: "James has gone to bed. He says he's got a headache and doesn't want to be distrubed." And at eleven, Grace Morland had been still alive.

James was saying to Pippi: "It was probably me that you saw in the orchard. I strolled down that way and was—er—walking about. Funny we didn't meet. Not that it matters in the least, but the police will ask."

"They have," said Pippi, and gave them a jocular wink.

The police continued to ask. Inspector Cockrill, with rims of sleeplessness round his birdlike bright eyes, cast his felt hat upon the stand in the hall (now reopened to the public), and led the way into Pendock's library, and questioned them each in turn. When that was over he summoned them all together, and made a short speech.

"Well, ladies and gentlemen, I won't keep you longer than I can help. This is a terrible affair, and you've all been very good in helping me to sort out the facts of it. As I see it now, the murder was committed between the hours of eleven, when Miss Morland was last seen alive by her maid, and midnight, when the body was discovered by the butler. In the meantime the hat had been removed from the hall here and was later found upon the body. I have evidence" (he glanced at Fran with an almost imperceptible wink) "that the box was on the hall-stand, and apparently undisturbed, at eleven o'clock. From that time onwards, the doors and windows were locked and bolted from the inside; and after the crime I found them still locked and bolted from the inside." He paused impressively and rolled himself a cigarette.

"It's im*poss*ible, Cockie," said Francesca. "And anyway, nobody *knew* about the hat."

"A great many people knew about it," corrected Cockie sternly. "You knew about it yourself. Lady Hart knew about it. Venetia and Mr. Gold and Captain Nicholl knew about it. Miss Morland herself knew about it. And the butler here knew about it."

"*And* all the rest of the servants no doubt," added Lady Hart.

He swung round upon her. "Ah, the servants! I thought we should soon come to the servants. Now, let me tell you, ladies and gentlemen, that the servants at Pigeonsford House have nothing to do with this crime. For a long time before eleven, and till some time after twelve, the cook was having a toothache; and a most providential toothache it turns out to be, for it kept them all running about with oil of cloves and hot towels and little nips of brandy, I shouldn't wonder, and anyway, well within each other's range of observation. None of them could have been absent long enough even to start on the murder. The butler certainly knew all about the hat; but at twenty or twenty-five minutes past eleven he was starting off from Tenfold to bicycle home; and if he did the four miles over the downs, through the snow which is still quite thick up there, lured the poor lady from her house, killed her, fetched the hat and put it on her head, and ran across the lawns to summon help—all in the space of thirty-five minutes, then all I can say is that he's a better man for his age than I am for mine." He glared at Bunsen as though he quite resented such an affront to his own physique. Bunsen gave him a grateful, tremulous smile.

"As for the old woman down at the Cottage," continued the Inspector, rolling himself another of his untidy cigarettes, "I suppose you'll admit that she's hardly in the picture." He looked round at their faces, as though there were the slightest possibility of their questioning it. "Well then. She's out. The butler's out. The servants are out. There remain six people who knew about the hat; and those six people, be*cause* they knew about the hat, must come under suspicion. I'm sorry, but you must face the facts. And those are the facts."

"But, Cockie, the *man*iac! The man who killed the girl last year in the wood."

"We're coming to the 'maniac,'" said Cockrill sourly. He added with an air of inconsequence: "You were all down here at the time, weren't you?"

"Yes, we were staying with Pen. And James was at 'The Black Dog' in the village."

"And Miss le May? Was she at the Cottage, do you remember?"

Lady Hart stared at him. "Why do you want to know all this?"

"Nothing, nothing, nothing; just asking." His mahogany-coloured fingers played with his cigarette. "But as a matter of interest—was she?"

"I don't know why we should be supposed to know anything about the le May girl's affairs, but actually I happen to remember that she wasn't. Was she, children? She was abroad with a touring company, and the only reason it sticks in my mind was that we heard she was having difficulty in getting back, because of the war." Her expression added that it was a pity she had ever succeeded.

"Oh. These two crimes," said Cockie in a new voice, staring thoughtfully at the cigarette. "It does look rather as though there were some connection, doesn't it?"

"Only that in both cases the heads were—cut off!"

"Isn't that enough?" said the Inspector, with sardonic amusement.

"Well, yes, of course. You mean that they must have been done by the same person?"

"Not must have been, Fran; may have been."

"But, Inspector, it's all so simple," protested Henry. "We decided that the murderer last summer was a tramp, a homicidal maniac. If the same man strikes again, why look for him at Pigeonsford House? Why start talking about us coming under suspicion?"

"If *you* decided that he was a tramp—and a maniac," said Cockie coolly, "that doesn't mean to say that the police did. He may have been, of course; but if he was a maniac he was a very unusual one, to say the least of it. The girl had been tied up and then decapitated with the scythe; most homicidal maniacs, whatever they may do afterwards, kill the victim with the hands, or with anything they may happen to have in their hands—they strangle or bludgeon or slash or stab. The lust to kill is strong and they don't waste time on fancy stuff like tying up the victim first. Furthermore, there was no sexual interference; that isn't extraordinary, of course, but it all adds up. And if, as you want to think, the man was a tramp, what is he doing here now? Tramps don't stay put. By the very nature of the beast, they move on."

"He might have moved full cycle and come back," suggested James, with a descriptive twiddle of his forefinger.

"He might," agreed Cockie amiably, but he did not look impressed.

Such little snow as had been lying on the ground on the evening before, had melted during the night, so that it was impossible to distinguish between footprints made before and after the crime. The head had been severed from the body with a large, rather blunt hatchet, which lay discarded at the edge of the drive. Sergeant Jenkins, extremely portentous, sought an interview with the owner of this hatchet.

"Er—relating to this matter of a 'atchet, left in the orchard outside Pigeonsford Cottage on the night before—well, last night: the police is seeking to establish the exact whereabouts of this 'atchet and the time it was left in the orchard outside Pigeonsford Cottage on the day before the . . ."

"You got the needle stuck," said the farmer's small boy, who, having been banished from the parlour upon the arrival of Sergeant Jenkins, now reappeared at the window. Jenkins frowned austerely.

"Left 'er there for choppin' up sticks the follering day," said the farmer heavily. He added truculently, for he was very much afraid: "Nothin' wrong in that, is ther? It's what I allus does."

"A very dangerous 'abit," said Sergeant Jenkins severely. "'Oo knew you was in the 'abit of leaving the 'atchet there?"

"Anybody might a known. Other 'and nobody need a known to have used it for the job. It was lying ther, just on the edge of the path, other side of the little bridge. She were an old 'atchet, all rusted up, and I didn't set no store by 'er. Just used 'er for breakin' up sticks. . . ."

Sergeant Jenkins pursued his investigations as far as Torrington, whence young Dr. Newsome had been summoned to minister to Bunsen's sister, at ten o'clock, the night before. Dr. Newsome, hopping with impatience, passed a hand over his crinkly gold hair, and confirmed that he had driven over to Tenfold, which lies between Torrington and Pigeonsford village, and visited the sick woman; that he had arranged for the district nurse to go to her, and that he had remained until the nurse arrived; that the patient's brother had

been there all the time, and that he would be very glad
if the sergeant would excuse him now as he was in the
devil of a hurry and already late on his rounds. The
nurse, in her turn, said that she had arrived at the little
cottage at about eleven o'clock, to find both Dr. Newsome and the patient's brother there; that the brother
had waited until she settled the old lady for the night,
and had finally left to bicycle back to Pigeonsford, at
about twenty past eleven, and that surely the sergeant
could let her go now, because if he was not busy, she
was, and could have told him the whole thing in five
minutes without spinning it out like this for half an
hour. . . .

Trotty had been, of all things, a trapeze artist, in the
buxom days of her youth. She had lived and worked,
and had been going to marry in the vital atmosphere of
the circus-ring, doing her job well though not bril-
liantly, her only spectacular performance her last. For
a single day Trotty's name had been big upon the
posters all over England; thenceforward she had
dragged herself through life with pitiful patched-up
legs. Grace Morland's mother had befriended her, as
she befriended all the broken hearts and broken bodies
that came her way; had given her some small job and
later taken her into her household, where she had remained to this day, faithful, devoted, grateful and increasingly crotchety. She was a downright, humorous,
ginger-haired little woman, her splendid muscle all run
to firm white fat. She received three visitors from the
'Ouse without fuss, and stood, clutching for support at
the back of a chair, while she spoke to them.

"Sit down, Trotty dear, do," said Venetia, getting a
chair and placing it for the old woman.

"Yes, Trotty, sit down." Pendock took her plump little hands in his own: "I'm so sorry for you in all this
trouble."

Her eyes filled with tears. "Poor dear Miss Grace;
what an end for her to come to, that always lived so
finicky and lady-like! I wanted to go to her, Mr. Pendock, sir; I don't like to think of her lying alone in

some cold place, with nobody she knows about her; but they won't let me see her. You couldn't arrange for me to see her, could you, sir?"

"Oh, Trotty, it's better not," said Fran quickly. "They've taken her away to—to the hospital, and they'll keep her there till we've had time to arrange for her funeral. It's a good thing you've got Pippi here, isn't it? She'll see to all that, and of course if there's anything in the world that any of us can do for you, you've only to let us know. You will, won't you?"

"Yes, Trotty; if you want any help, you've only to send for me. I'm sure you know that."

"Everybody in Pigeonsford knows that, Mr. Pendock," she said sincerely. "It was good of you to come down and see me, sir; and the young ladies."

They talked for a little while. Pendock said at last, diffidently: "Trotty—I wanted to ask you something; about this hat? Has the Inspector asked you about a hat?"

"He's been on and on about it," said Trotty, with a puzzled air. "Miss Grace never told me anything about any hat, Mr. Pendock. What does it matter, when my poor lady's lying killed and murdered, about some miserable hat? None of Miss Grace's hats is missing, that I do know."

"It was my hat," said Fran, as though she were a little ashamed to admit it.

"Didn't Miss Morland mention it to you when she came in last night, Trotty? She didn't like it at all, she thought it was a silly little hat, and I expect she told you about it and said what she thought of it . . . ?"

"She never mentioned it, sir. And I can tell you why I'm so certain; she went straight to her room when she came down from the 'Ouse. She called out that she'd had her tea, and up she went, and didn't come down till Miss Pippi arrived, just before eight o'clock. I thought she'd been crying; but with the excitement of Miss Pippi coming, I didn't worry any more about it, and she certainly didn't say anything about any hat, and she didn't say nothing to Miss Pippi either. I was with them all the time, getting them some supper and then standing by while Miss Pippi was telling about her doings in the revue and all. I like to 'ear about them things, Mr. Pendock, it puts me in mind of the old days; and Miss Pippi's very kind, she was telling all the jokes and adventures, and I know it was mostly to please me. Miss Grace doesn't really approve of those sort of things; she shuts her mind to the broader things of life, messing about with paints and embroidery and forgetting that paint can be used on the outsides of houses, and that there's such a thing as coarse, warm, necessary clothes without any frills or fancies; though God forgive me for seeming to say a word against her, for she was a good kind mistress to me, and now she's dead, poor thing."

"And never having said a word about the hat?"

"Not a word, Miss Venetia. Some time after ten Miss Pippi said she was stuffy and she'd like to go out for some air. Miss Grace she keeps the drawing-room rather warm, you know, and Miss Pippi she's used to theatrical life, with all its draughts and chills and seldom enough a nice cosy sit by the fire; so Miss Grace went up to bed and I cleared the meal away. It's as true as I stand here, sir," said Trotty earnestly, sitting on a chair, "that Miss Grace never mentioned that hat. Never *men*tioned the hat."

"But later on, when Pippi came in again?"

"Miss Pippi came in just before eleven, Miss Fran, and went up to her room. I followed her upstairs and saw her into bed. Then I took Miss Grace's drink to her room; she was standing there without a light, looking out of the window, and she was queer, Mr. Pendock. She said she'd got somebody in the 'ollow of her hand; but she never said nothing at all about the hat."

"And that was the last time you saw her?"

"It was, sir. I went back to Miss Pippi to take her empty cup, and was talking to her and listening to her tales until she'd finished her drink, and for a long time after that; it must have been well after half-past eleven when I went downstairs and to my bed. . . ."

Their hopes began to fall. "And you didn't go out? You didn't go down to the village and talk to anyone there?"

"Go out?" said Trotty, amazed. "No, indeed, Miss Fran. What would I be going out for at that time of night, me that can hardly walk so far by the light of day? If you think I've been talking, Miss, I can tell you you're wrong. I saw nobody but Miss Grace and Miss Pippi last night, and Miss Grace never told either of us nothing about no hat."

They had never suspected her of doing more than spread the story of the hat; to suppose for a moment that this frail old woman with her crippled legs and painful, dragging walk could have murdered her mistress, was as ludicrous as it was repellent; and anyway, now it seemed that she had not known of the hat. Bunsen was Out. And Trotty was Out. And Pippi had not been told about the hat.

That afternoon they went for a walk, straggling in twos and threes along the bank of the little stream that runs between Pigeonsford Cottage and the 'Ouse. Pippi le May saw them from the window of her bedroom and called to them to wait for her; she ran after them, bright and bouncing, with her cap of coarse auburn hair and her expensive little suit that somehow looked rather cheap.

Francesca walked with Lady Hart, subduing her young strides to the old lady's ponderous roll. "I say— Gran."

"Yes, darling?" said Lady Hart, rather surprised, for Fran usually said all in a rush, whatever was in her mind.

"Do you like James?"

"Yes, I do. I like him very much."

"So do I," said Fran doubtfully.

"What you mean is that you don't know whether you like him enough to marry him."

"Well, actually, darling, it's more than that. I like him most terribly; I won't say that I'm madly in love with him, but Venetia says it's more comfortable not to be."

"Because Venetia's uncomfortably in love with *her* husband, it doesn't follow that it's the same for everyone," said Lady Hart, smiling lovingly after the little shining figure that walked ahead of them. "The lucky people get it half and half."

"Well, I know, Gran, but never mind about that. Suppose I do love James enough to marry him and James loves me—which, as a matter of fact, he does . . . well . . . would you say that he was a good person for me to marry? I mean the right person, really the best for me?"

Lady Hart considered. "This is very important, Fran; but yes, I think I do. We've known James a long time now, on and off, ever since he was a boy; he's well off and he's in a good social position, so that part of it's all right, but the great thing is that he's good and charming and has what the Eastern religions call 'compassion,' and I don't think he could do anything cruel or crooked if he tried. He's terribly vague, of course, and sometimes he's rather irritating, because he looks as if he were sound asleep when you're talking to him and you get careless and silly and say worthless things, and all the time he's awake and summing you up; but if you love him, darling, and he really loves you . . ."

"He loves me most terribly, Granny," said Francesca in a subdued small voice. "It's quite—I don't know—— You say yourself how sleepy and casual he seems; well, when he wakes up it's—it quite takes your breath away. It's rather a sort of responsibility to have someone loving you as much as all that. . . ."

Lady Hart could understand. There was something about Fran that turned your heart upside-down for her, even if you were only her grandmother. She was so young and fresh and pretty, and always with that sort of gallantry about her, that resolution to fight her own battles against the world and never show where, in the soft, deep places of her heart, she might be hurt or afraid. A man in love with her beauty and gaiety must feel also a tremendous tenderness, a longing to protect her from harm, to wrap her about with kindness and gentleness. . . . She said quietly: "Only you can know how much you care for James, Fran darling. But if you do—I think he's the man for you."

They walked for a moment in silence, Fran with her head bent, looking at her little shoes. She said at last: "I say, Gran. You know Pippi le May . . . ?"

"What has Pippi le May got to do with this?" said Lady Hart sharply.

It took Fran a long time to tell her what Pippi le May had to do with it.

Pippi caught up with Pendock and walked between him and James. "I hear you've been telling the police that I was on tour last summer. They're poking about for proofs. Fortunately nothing could be simpler, because they can check up with the manager of the company I was with. I never left the show for a day. But why this thusness, do you think?"

"They're doing it to all of us," said Pendock indifferently.

"I suppose it's because of that girl that was slain in the copse near the Cottage. Do they connect her up with poor old Grace?"

"They have to look into it, anyway."

"Because if they do, it lets me out; that is if they're trying to make out that I bumped the poor old girl off for the sake of her pinchbeck bracelet and a painting of the Church Tower in Blossom Time, which is what she's always told me I get by her will. Anyway, I'm safe enough, because I certainly didn't know anything about Fran's famous hat. Do you think they suspect me?"

"I don't think they suspect you or any of us," said Pendock irritably. "It's all the routine stuff."

"All right, all right, all right; just asking!" said Pippi, quoting Inspector Cockrill.

James Nicholl walked beside her, saying not a word. "Is Venetia calling you?" said Pippi suddenly, to Pendock.

He went back, leaving the two of them together. "Did you call me, Venetia?"

"No," said Venetia, surprised.

"Now that you're here," said Henry in his eager way, "stay and talk to us. We've been going over and over things, and you know, Pendock, you really can't get away from the fact that it looks as if one of us . . . ."

"*Or* Pippi," said Venetia firmly.

"Or Pippi—as if one of us six, or Pippi, may have done this frightful affair of Grace Morland. I know it seems fantastic," said Henry hastily, "but look at it fair and square: who else could it have been? I can't see that the business of the hat can have been just chance; *or* the ditch. I mean, dash it all, the woman said she wouldn't be seen dead in a ditch in the hat, and a few hours later she was. You can't get away from it."

"Some maniac . . ." insisted Pendock.

"That's what I've been saying," said Venetia sadly; "but as Henry says—why the hat?—and why the ditch? There's acres of ground round Pigeonsford, and only one poor little ditch: why did the maniac put the body there? Not to hide it, because it wasn't hidden— Bunsen saw it at once. Darling—honestly, the coincidence is too much."

"Well, but what about the girl last summer? That was a maniac obviously: there was literally no motive. . . ."

"If that's your only reason for thinking it was a maniac, the same applies to Miss Morland: after all, the poor woman was harmless enough."

"Just what I say: the maniac was responsible for both."

"But put it another way, Pendock; allow for a minute that only someone who knew about the hat—and that means one of us—could have murdered Miss Morland; well, couldn't that person have murdered the kitchen-maid, too?"

"Oh, Henry darling—*no*!"

"But it's true, Venetia; after all, if we're going to acknowledge that one of us could do the one—why not the other? It was no more horrible. . . ."

"But we don't acknowledge it; it's only that that wretched hat . . ."

"The police are taking the hat pretty seriously," said Henry.

"But they don't know about Grace Morland's remark—about being seen dead in a ditch, I mean."

"You don't think we ought to tell them, do you?" suggested Henry, going off at a tangent.

"Good God, no," said Pendock violently.

"Ah, but that's the point," said Venetia sadly. "Why not? If you think we're all so safe and innocent, what's wrong with telling them? The truth is," she added, wagging her golden head, walking along beside Henry, tightly holding his hand, "the truth is that you're afraid to tell them. And so'm I. And so's Henry. Aren't you, Henry?"

"Terrified," admitted Henry readily.

"If we were another lot of people—I mean not you, Pen, and Henry and me and Granny and Fran and James—well, we wouldn't hesitate, would we? We'd think it was all quite clear, wouldn't we, that some one of us six who heard Grace say that, had, for some reason unknown, killed her and put the hat on her head? It's only because we're *us* that we blind ourselves to the facts."

The air was cold and clear, with promise of fresh snow; the stream ran, willow-bordered, upon their right; in the distance a train whistled like some shrill mechanical bird, and a puff of dark smoke hung motionless over the snowy downs. They walked for a while in silence. Henry said, smiling his puckish smile: "If only it could be Pippi!"

"It's not Pippi," said Pendock definitely. "It's almost impossible that there isn't some connection between the two deaths; and Pippi was not here when the kitchen-maid was killed last summer. It isn't Pippi."

They were silent again, each withdrawn into himself; behind them Lady Hart and Fran walked, also in silence; ahead, Pippi le May was talking to James volubly, waving expressive hands. Venetia said at last bitterly: "She doesn't care two hoots about her cousin;

we didn't go much on old Morland, but I think we feel it more than Pippi. If only it could have been her!"

"I suppose I'd better ask her in to dinner tonight," said Pendock with a sigh, for he did not care at all for Pippi le May.

Pippi accepted with alacrity, and at seven o'clock walked up from the Cottage, fur-coated, with a bright woollen scarf tied over her head and wound about her throat. Pendock intercepted one of the housemaids on the landing: "Oh, Gladys, I want to arrange for one of you girls to go down and sit with Trotty at the Cottage while Miss le May's up here; ask Bunsen to see to it, will you?"

Gladys was a fine young woman with excessively curly hair and stout, round legs; she cherished a secret passion for her employer, and now said eagerly: "I'll go myself, sir—if you'd like me to."

Pendock did not care two hoots who went; he said indifferently: "All right, Gladys; if that suits Bunsen, you go."

Gladys, however, was not going to lose so splendid an opportunity of making herself interesting. She said, with a show of timidity, that she didn't know if she could, after all, bring herself to pass the—to go near the—she was afraid she was ever so silly but she really was too——

"What are you talking about, child?" said Pendock patiently.

Gladys was talking about the spot where Miss Morland had been killed, but it was not to be expected that she would explain this in so many words. Pendock said at last: "Well, get one of the men to walk down with you; and go across the lawn, then you needn't pass near the drive. And try and be a sensible girl and don't talk this kind of talk to the others . . . you'll have them all upset."

Gladys explained that her nerves had been bad from a child.

It seemed dreadful to be standing round a big fire in the beautiful, familiar drawing-room, drinking cocktails, when Miss Morland, who had sat and had tea there the day before, was lying in a mortuary, murdered and mutilated; but what could one do about it? Fran said, in that ruthless way of hers that hid so much of delicacy and pain and pity: "We couldn't go anywhere else, Pen, could we? And we need drinks more than ever, just because of it . . . to try and shut out the idea of her . . . poor Miss Morland. . . ."

"I keep thinking of her too," said Venetia, who knew the innermost workings of Fran's heart. "It's so impossible to believe that here, in Pen's garden, she should have died, and died like—that. But it doesn't do *her* any good to brood over it; and it's only worse for us." She added: "I'm so sorry, Pippi . . . we shouldn't be talking about it in front of you."

Pippi looked blank. "Oh, good heavens, don't mind about me. I mean, it's rotten about poor old Grace, but there's no use moaning over it, is there?"

Pendock looked at her with increasing dislike. Odd how people could say almost the same things and have such different meanings. Fran and Venetia, he knew, were haunted by their own imaginary reconstructions of the scene in the moonlight, down by the drive; he himself could not blot it from his mind—though, strangely enough, the first death, that of the girl in the wood, remained more clearly with him; but Pippi seemed genuinely not to care at all, to be able to continue her own heedless way, cocky, impregnable, tough. He finished his drink at a gulp and said abruptly: "Let's go in to dinner."

The Inspector burst in upon them as they sat round the table. "Sorry to disturb you, Mr. Pendock, but I'm off for the night. They've taken a man into custody at Torrington, and I'll have to go and see him. I'll leave someone here in case you need them, but I don't think you will." He was about to rush off when the news that had been oozing out of him suddenly emerged with a plop: "This man has confessed to the murder of that girl last summer," he said, and was gone.

A load seemed to lift from about their hearts and Pendock expressed the feelings of everybody at the table when he said over his shoulder to Bunsen: "I think we'll have some champagne."

Pippi was used to cocktails but not to champagne. It warmed the cockles of her heart and went straight to her henna'ed head. "I know you all thought it was me," she said cheerfully, waving her golden glass. "But you see you were wrong. It was this nasty ole tramp."

"We didn't think it was you at all," said Fran, who was, indeed, innocent of any such charge. "It couldn't have been you, because you couldn't have known about the hat."

"Ah, but thasswhere you were wrong," said Pippi, giggling joyously.

"Trotty definitely told us that she was with you and Miss Morland all the evening," said Pendock, staring at her. "And that Miss Morland said nothing to either of you about the hat."

"Quirright," said Pippi. She was only just drunk enough to make her enjoy a pretence of being more drunk than she actually was.

"Then you couldn't have known. No one could have known."

"Anyone could have known," corrected Pippi. She nodded her head at them artfully. "*I* could have known; tramp could have known; anybody could have known."

"I don't see what you mean, Pippi," said Venetia, leaning across the big table with the candlelight on her hair. "The story didn't go out of this house; and if Miss Morland didn't tell anyone . . ."

"How do you know she didn't tell anyone?"

"But who could she have told?" said Venetia, bewildered by her air of jaunty triumph; and Fran, from the other end of the table, chimed in impatiently: "When could she have told them?"

"She could have told them just before she died," said Pippi, and drained her glass and set it down with a thump. "She could have told her murderer."

She could have told her murderer. This man, this creature who had confessed to killing the kitchen-maid; he had somehow lured Grace out of her house and she, for some reason they would probably never know, had told him about the hat. And after he had killed her he had got the hat and thrust it upon her head; how he could have got it, why she should have told him, were questions for the police to answer; it was sufficient to know that there was a self-confessed murderer to account for the incredible horrors of the night before and that they were safe. Lady Hart and Fran and Venetia and Henry and James were safe. And Pippi, of course—but who cared for Pippi le May? Pendock leant back in his chair, sick and dizzy with the relief of it.

Strong black coffee brought Pippi back to normal; she was unashamed of her lapse into insobriety and chattered away full of herself and her doings until Pendock, his head now aching violently, could bear it no longer. Lady Hart was silent and distrait, and he saw that Pippi was getting badly on her nerves. He said at last: "I think the snow's getting heavier. I hate to speed the parting guest, Miss le May, but you wouldn't want to get cut off from the Cottage, would you?"

"I shouldn't mind in the least," said Pippi, laughing.

"Well, no, of course, we could always put you up; but my housemaid is down there with Trotty, and she's got to get home."

Pippi could hardly ignore so broad a hint; she swathed her head in the scarf and wriggled into her cheap little ocelot coat. "Come on, then; who's going to see me home?"

"I am, of course," said Pendock, unhooking his coat from the stand in the hall.

"Remember what happened to the last person you saw home!" said Pippi brightly. At the sight of their faces she had the grace to look ashamed of herself, and added apologetically: "Oh, well, I'm sorry; perhaps that was rather an unfortunate remark." She went on, turning to Pendock: "But honestly, don't bother to come. I shan't get mislaid between here and the Cottage, and the snow's not quite at the lost-for-days-in-a-drift stage."

"Of course I'm coming," said Pendock testily; but as he caught her arm and marched her out in the middle of her farewells, he saw something in her face that all of them had missed that night: a shadow of weariness, of loneliness, perhaps of fear, under the cocky smile, and for the first time he warmed to her a little and said apologetically: "I'm sorry, my dear; I'm afraid I've been rather abrupt. It's been a dreadful day, and, of course, last night . . ."

"It must have been a shock for you especially," said Pippi, more gently than he had ever heard her speak.

"I thought it was Fran," he explained, as though he were telling her for the first time, as though she had not heard, over and over again, the details of last night's discovery. "God help me, I thought it was Fran. I ran through the hall and down these very steps and out over the grass, and all the time I was thinking that I should find Fran there in the ditch, with her head hacked off her body. . . ." He shuddered violently and buried his face in his hands.

Pippi said nothing, and they continued on their way in silence. Gladys, all of a dither at the thought of walking home with the master, opened the door to them. "Where's Trotty?" said Pippi, looking past her into the little hall.

"She's gone off to bed, Miss. She was ever so tired, and she thought you wouldn't mind. I took her a nice cup of milk. . . ." ('The girl's sweet smile and kindly thought quite won the heart of the proud, rich man,' thought Gladys, showing all her teeth for the benefit of Pendock.) "I tucked her up comfortable. . . ."

Pippi was searching in her handbag and through the pockets of her coat. "Dash it—I believe I've left my gigs up at the house; I'll have to come back with you and get them."

"Will you want them to-night?" said Pendock.

"My dear, yes, I *must;* I mean I can't read a word without them. . . ."

"Is it your glasses, Miss?" said Gladys, returning in her best coat from the kitchen quarters. "Because Trotty found them on the droring-room mantelpiece, and she took them up to your room; she said you'd want them if you were going to read in bed."

"Oh, good! Thank you, Gladys." She looked out at the driving snow and said, with the careless good-nature of her kind: "Here, you'd better have my scarf. Wind it round your head and tuck it over your chest; you can let me have it back to-morrow—no hurry." She stood in the doorway and called: "Good-night. God bless."

Pendock was silent on the walk home. In the hall he said to the girl: "Better leave the scarf here; I shall be seeing Miss le May to-morrow, I expect, or anyway I'll arrange that she gets it back."

"Yes, sir. All right, sir. And thanks ever so much for seeing me home, sir."

Pendock was practically unaware that he had seen Gladys home; but he smiled at her in his kindly way and said, "Good-night, my child."

'. . . and that moonlight walk through the snow set the seal on the beautiful housemaid's romance,' thought Gladys joyfully.

Fran and Venetia and Henry and James were playing Vingt-et-un. "Weren't we fools to start this?" said Venetia, laughing. We shall go on all night. But we had to get the taste of Pippi out of our mouths."

"Where's your grandmother?" said Pendock.

"Here I am," called Lady Hart; the writing bureau was out of sight in the short end of the L-shaped drawing room. "I'm struggling with a letter to the Income Tax people and I wish to be left severely alone. How do you spell preposterous?"

"Come and play Vingt-et," said Fran, holding out her hand to Pendock. She felt rather shy of him now that she had had a glimpse of his passion for her, and especially since her talk in the orchard with James.

Venetia looked under the table. "Aziz; oh, you *are* there, darling! I thought he must have gone out when Pen opened the door."

Pendock stood beside Fran, holding her hand in his own warm grasp, and watched the game for a moment. "I don't think I'll play. I've still got an awful head. It's," he glanced at the clock, "eleven o'clock and I want to get some sleep to-night."

"Well, it's a pity, darling, because we should have had to divide up a bit, and Henry could have given you some of his money. Look at him, he's got so many matches that we've had to give him a lump sum of James's lighter, and distribute them again."

"Trust a Jew," said Venetia, laughing. "He always does it. It only shows that it's quite right when they say that the Jews have all the money and people like Henry are responsible for the War and Mussolini and the measles epidemic and the common cold and everything else that ever goes wrong with the world. . . ."

"Well, I absolve him from responsibility for my headache," said Pendock. "Did you ever hear anyone talk like that le May girl? Oh, and by the way, she lent Gladys her scarf, so will someone see that she gets it back to-morrow? She's sure to be up here sometime. I've put it in the left-hand little drawer of the stand in the hall."

"I'll take it down to the Cottage in the morning," said James, indolently dealing out cards. "I ought to go and pay my respects to Trotty."

"Will you? Thanks very much. Well, I'm off to bed," said Pendock, with his hand on the door handle. "Thank God we can all sleep a bit more easily to-night. Good-night, my children. Good-night, Lady Hart."

"Good-night," called Lady Hart's voice from around the corner. "Sleep well!" They could hear her pen, scratching away as she wrote.

CHAPTER 4

Pendock was dreaming again; he saw the same dim tunnel stretching out before him, the woman standing at the end of it, out in the sunshine, and felt the same strange urge to see her face. He put his hand beneath her chin to lift her head, and there came again the thunderous din in the tunnel behind him; he swung round to see what had made it, and when he turned back again, the woman was gone. Hands reached out of the tunnel and caught him by the shoulders . . . a voice said urgently: "Wake up, wake up, wake up!"

He was awake and shivering, sick with foreboding and fear. The man leaning over him was Cockrill.

"For God's sake—what is it?" said Pendock.

"Get up, man; I thought you'd never wake. Fran's room—quick, which is her room?"

"Over there, opposite mine, across the corridor. Why do you want Fran's room . . . ?"

But Cockrill was across the passage and flinging open Fran's door. Pendock pushed him aside and ran to the bed. "Francesca! Oh, God! Oh, Christ! Fran darling——"

Cockrill felt for the switch and turned on the light. She was lying in her bed as she had been the morning before, her dark hair spread softly over the pillow, her heavy eyelashes curling against her cheek; but this time she was really asleep. He caught her by the shoulder, and laid his face against her hair, holding her to his heart. "My darling, thank God you're safe."

Aziz leapt down from an arm-chair, barking anxiously. Fran stirred and woke up. "What on earth— Pen! Good lord, what's happening now?"

Lady Hart appeared in the doorway, white-faced, with soft, untidy hair. Soon they were all in Fran's room, Venetia clinging to her sister, James looking increasingly vague and sleepy as Cockrill's story unfolded itself, his face as grey as a ghost's. A sergeant came to the door and reported stolidly: "All safe in the servants' quarters, sir."

"Good. Well, now, get as many men as you can around the house. Have someone on the landing out here and put a man on the terrace below the windows of this room; and send Troot here."

"Outside my room?" cried Fran, fightened and bewildered. "Why my room? What is all this about?"

"I'm afraid you've been in some danger, young lady," said Cockie, looking at her almost angrily from beneath his beetling brows; "but don't worry now. You'll be safe enough; we'll look after you."

Lady Hart sat down heavily on the edge of her granddaughter's bed. "Cockie—you must tell us what's happened. You can't leave us in this uncertainty. Why should Fran be in danger?"

The Inspector produced a tin of tobacco and some papers and rolled one of his wispy cigarettes; he stood there looking down at it, and his nicotined fingers were shaking as they worked. He said at last: "I received a telephone call an hour ago from this house. A woman's voice spoke to me. She said: 'Francesca's next.'"

"A woman—what woman?" cried Fran.

"Well, she said she was the murderer," said Cockie, and lighted his cigarette.

A second policeman arrived in the doorway of Fran's room. "You sent for me, sir?"

"Yes, Troot. You've been on duty here since I left this evening?"

"Yessir."

"What were the various people in this house doing at eleven o'clock?"

"At eleven o'clock, sir? The ladies and gentlemen were in the droring-room and the servants they was in the servants' 'all."

"All the servants?"

"Yes, sir. Not counting the gardeners, but they live

out in the village. All the rest was there, except Mr. Bunsen, sir. I let him in just a few minutes ago; he'd been over to Tenfold, sir."

"Yes, yes, he had permission to go. But the others were all together?"

"Yessir. A young woman, the housemaid, sir, she'd just come back from sitting with the maid at the Cottage. The rest of the staff waited up to 'ear if there was any titbits of news, like. . . . I saw Mr. Pendock go down with Miss le May, sir, but I wasn't to know that he bring the girl back with 'im, and I knew she was a bit nervous; so I went into the kitchen quarters after Mr. Pendock went into the droring-room, just before eleven, to see if she'd got back safe and sound. I was there about 'alf an hour, and nobody left the kitching during that time."

"You're certain of it?"

"Oh yes, sir, certain. The talk was rather free, like, over a cup of coffee, and I thought I might learn something if I stayed on. I was there till they went up to bed. After that I made a tour of the 'ouse to see that everything was locked up proper. . . ."

"Yes, yes, never mind about that. Now, Mr. Pendock, where are the telephones in this house?"

"There's one in the hall," said Pendock—"that's the main one; the other two are extensions, one to the library and one to the servants' hall."

"Which was under my heye, sir," said the constable.

"And, Mr. Pendock, where were you and your guests between eleven o'clock and eleven-fifteen to-night— last night," corrected Cockie, taking out his watch.

"We were all in the drawing-room," said Pendock thankfully.

"*All?*"

"Yes, certainly. These four were playing Vingt-et-un, and Lady Hart was writing letters, and I stood talking to them till some time after eleven."

Cockie manœuvred into position and clicked on the switch of Fran's electric fire with his toe. "Oh. Can you be sure of the time?"

Pendock looked doubtful. "Yes, don't you re-member," said Henry suddenly, "you said it was eleven o'clock and you were going to bed? I glanced at the drawing-room clock as you said it, and it was just a minute or two after eleven."

"Is that clock right?"

"Yes, it's one of those electric things."

"Oh," said Cockie again, looking anything but pleased. He added to Pendock: "And did you, in fact, go to bed?"

"Yes, I did. I talked for two or three minutes longer——"

"What do you mean by two or three. Two? Or three? Or four or five?"

"I mean two—or three—or four or five. I honestly can't remember any nearer than that. I stood and talked to them for a few minutes after I had looked at the clock, and then I said good-night and went up-stairs."

"And after that?" said Cockrill to the others.

Lady Hart got up from Fran's bed and sat down in the big arm-chair. "I was writing letters at the desk. At about half-past eleven or a little later—now don't start your two or three or five business with *me,* Cockie, because I don't know nearer than that—I finished my letter and got it passed by Henry and James, and then I sat with the children for a while and watched their game. I don't know if you know Vingt-et-un, Inspector, but it's apt to go on for two or three—or four or five— days, if you let it. Henry had been winning rather heav-ily but he began to lose again, and I persuaded them that it would never end and they'd better go up to bed. We'd had rather a terrible night the night before, and I thought they should all get some sleep and try to forget it." She added gently, looking at their anxious faces: "Life doesn't stand still, even when murders and mys-teries force themselves into the lives of ordinary peo-ple like ourselves. Things seem to go on much as usual, and you talk and eat and get on with your every-day life, because there's nothing else to be done about it, but it's all in your mind, and it's rather a strain. I think that's why they were playing Vingt-et-un."

"You ought to be a sob-sister on the Daily Whatsaname, darling, said Fran, but she smiled at her lovingly.

"What time is it?" said Henry suddenly.

"It's well after midnight," said Cockrill. "I got over as quickly as I could, but Torrington's fifteen miles, and it's the devil driving through these country lanes with the blackout lighting, not to mention the snow. Anyway, we were in good time," he smiled at Fran, "and don't worry, my dear, you'll be safe enough now we're here." Out came the tobacco tin again. "But as for that 'phone call—that's a puzzle, that is." He swung round suddenly upon Pendock. "I want you to say something to me in a woman's voice. Say: 'I'm speaking from Pigeonsford House.'"

Pendock opened his mouth and shut it again, looking foolish. "Good heavens, I *can't,* Inspector." He opened his mouth again and had another try, but no sound came. "It won't work," he said, laughing.

"Come on, come on," said Cockie irritably, lighting the new cigarette from the old one. "This is a murder case; we haven't got time for silly self-consciousness. Say something in as feminine a voice as you can manage."

It was a long time since Pendock had been spoken to in this tone, and for a moment indignation smouldered in the blue-green eyes; but he saw what the little man was driving at, and opening his mouth once more he said, in a ludicrous squeak: "I'm speaking from Pidg . . ." and broke down, laughing apologetically. "I'm awfully sorry, Inspector."

"Don't do it so loud," said Cockrill, maintaining an irritated gravity. "Try and imitate a woman, speaking very low; come on, now—'I'm speaking from Pigeonsford . . .'"

Pendock tried again. "Mr. Gold, you have a shot," said Cockie, paying no further attention to him.

Henry gave his whole mind to it, as he gave it to everything he did. There was a twinkle in his eye, but he said, perfectly seriously, in a low, soft voice: "I'm speaking from Pigeonsford House."

"Nicholl."

"Who—me?" said James, waking up.

"Try it, please."

"I'm speaking from Pigeonsford House," squeaked James without a smile.

Inspector Cockrill went over to the dressing-table and flicked his ash into the lid of Fran's powder-bowl. "Mr. Gold—what time did you leave the drawing-room?"

"I left with the others, whatever time that was. If you mean did I go to the telephone some time just after eleven and imitate a woman's voice, that won't wash; between half-past ten and half-past eleven, I was with at least four other people."

"And all the other people were with *him*, if you see what I mean," said Fran eagerly, sitting curled up in the middle of the bed, wrapped in the eiderdown. "So if you think it was any of us, well, it obviously wasn't."

"Can anybody swear to the exact time that Mr. Pendock left the drawing-room?" asked Cockie, ignoring her and steadily pursuing his own line of argument; and as nobody answered: "Was it ten past?"

"Just about," said Pendock.

"Just about—just about! I'm not interested in just-abouts. Was it five past?"

"No," said everybody at once.

"It was after five past?"

"Yes, definitely," they said. "*Defi*nitely."

But at five past eleven the unknown caller had been already on the telephone; he, or she, had insisted upon speaking to no one but himself, and it had taken a little time to locate him. The conversation had ended at eight minutes past eleven . . . the call must have been put through at eleven or almost immediately after. Besides, Cockrill thought he would have known if Pendock had not honestly been trying to imitate a woman's voice just now: you couldn't count too much on your instinct on these occasions, but it did mean a lot. He looked at them all quite fiercely. "Is everyone here present ready to swear," he said, "ready to *swear*, I say, in a court of law, as you well may have to do, that the five of you—Lady Hart and the two girls and James Nicholl and Mr. Gold—were together in the drawing-room downstairs from before eleven o'clock till at least half-past?"

Everybody nodded assent.

"And that Mr. Pendock was with you till at least some minutes after five past eleven, even possibly till ten past?"

They might have been Chinese mandarins.

"And there is nobody in this house except the servants and yourselves?"

"Nobody," said Pendock positively.

"Then I must be out of my mind," said Cockie, and crushed out his second cigarette and sent it into the waste-paper basket, after the first. He stumped across the room towards the door, pushing-to the door of the wall-cupboard as he went. "You'd better all go to bed and get some sleep. Sorry, Fran, I seem to have made rather a mess round your fireplace."

"It's all right, Cockie, pet," said Fran, craning over the end of the bed to look at the scattered ash. "Better than in my powder-box, anyway."

"Well, come along then. Everybody to your rooms, please."

"I'll stay with Fran," said Lady Hart, not moving from her chair.

"Fran's perfectly safe, Lady Hart. I'd rather you went back to your room."

Fran was about to protest, but could not bear to seem lily-livered. "Good heavens, I'll be all right. I mean, a man outside the window and another one outside the door, what more could a girl want—except perhaps one of them inside the room instead of out . . . ?"

"Let *me* stay with her, Cockie," pleaded Venetia.

Cockrill was worried, and when he was worried he was irritable. "Go back to your rooms," he said impatiently, "and do as I tell you. Francesca will be all right. Mr. Pendock, I'm afraid I'll have to keep you up a bit longer, and then we'd both better try and get some sleep."

"There's a sofa in the library," said Pendock, as they followed the rest of the party out on to the landing. "I'll bring down some rugs and things and you'll be quite comfortable there; sorry there isn't a spare bed to offer you. If you go down, I'll catch you up in a minute."

"I'll wait for you here," said Cockrill firmly, standing at the head of the stairs.

Pendock looked a little silly. "All right. But—do you mind if I say good-night to Fran? I won't be a minute."

The Inspector glanced at him sharply. He walked between the closed doors of the other bedrooms and knocked at Fran's. "Francesca—if you're not in bed, would you come to the door for a minute? Mr. Pendock would like to speak to you." As Fran appeared at the door he moved back two or three paces and said briefly: "There you are—go ahead."

Pendock eyed him, startled. "Good God, Cockie— surely you don't think—— I'm sorry," he said to Fran; "I just wanted to say good-night and ask you if there was anything you'd like me to do about—all this. I'll sit outside your door, if you like."

"Good lord, no, Pen darling. There's a man on the landing and I'll be as safe as houses now that the police are here. I'm not a bit frightened, honestly I'm not," said Fran in a quavering voice.

"I'll stay awake all night, darling, and keep my door open, just across the way. If there's the least thing you want . . ."

"No, truly, Pen, I'm fine. I'm quite all right. Don't stay awake—but thank you very much, darling, all the same.

He caught her hand. The Inspector moved a step nearer, but Pendock ignored him. His voice was shaking as much as Francesca's. He said: "Fran—before you go, give me a little kiss."

She put her hands up to his shoulders and, holding him lightly, kissed him on the lips. He was shaken with longing to catch her close to him, to take her into his arms and hold her safe for ever against his heart, but he returned her innocent kiss and let her go. Her face smiled up at him as she softly closed the door. He made uncertainly for the stairs.

"Rugs," said Cockrill gently.

"Oh yes. Rugs. Sorry, I forgot all about them. Rugs, rugs, rugs. . . ." He stood for a moment in a sort of blinding glory; and then, returning to sanity, went to a chest on the landing and took out an armful of blankets and led the way downstairs. "What about a drink?" he said.

"I could do with a Scotch," acknowledged Cockie gratefully. "It wasn't much fun getting here, I can assure you. The snow had stopped, but there was quite a lot in the lanes, and we couldn't see the road from the ditch. We got stuck once and had to heave her out; and all the time I was in a funk about Fran Hart."

"Why didn't you telephone?" said Pendock. "We could at least have looked after her until you got here."

"We couldn't get through. Lines must be down with the snow—and yet, dash it, it's only been falling for a couple of hours. I wonder." He turned back and went to the telephone in the corner of the big dim hall. The leaded wires that came through the small high window and across to the box were gashed through, and a pair of pruning-scissors lay on the sill. Cockie nodded with a little grimace, as who should say "Good Lord!" He said to Pendock: "We shall test both 'phones for fingerprints, but we shan't find a thing. It looks as if this were the one she used."

"She couldn't have been using it when I came out of the drawing-room," said Pendock, thinking back. "I used the door nearest the library, not the one in the L; but I'd certainly have seen her."

"I wonder would you have heard her from the drawing-room?" said Cockrill, judging the distance between the telephone and the drawing-room doors. "She spoke very low, of course."

"Oh, I don't think we need have heard," said Pendock, as they went on into the library. "The walls are tremendously thick as you can see, and the doors are heavy and solid. It's a very sound-proof house; it was built in the days when things were made strong and sturdy; and, for example, I never hear guests arriving at the front door. I don't think we need have heard her, definitely I don't." He added suddenly: "But now that I think of it—while I was talking in there, Venetia did look round for the dog. She said—what the devil did she say . . . ? That she thought he must have got out when I came in, or something like that. Perhaps she had heard something in the hall?"

Cockie was very much excited by this recollection and was only with difficulty restrained from dashing up to Venetia's room to have it corroborated. "But don't you *see*? She may actually have heard the woman speaking from the hall, or passing through here to the library to use this 'phone!"

"Well, she won't be able to tell you any more than I have," said Pendock, pushing him down on to the sofa, and thrusting a glass of whisky into his hand. "She can't have heard anything but the faintest possible sound, because she was perfectly satisfied as soon as she saw the dog." He poured himself out a drink and sat down at the other end of the sofa.

"All right," said Cockie, taking an enormous gulp. "We'll leave it till the morning. Now, Pendock, about the front door: I understand that you see to its being locked?"

"Yes, I do. Bunsen shuts up the rest of the house but I always see to that."

"And did you lock it after you when you came in from seeing Miss le May home?"

Pendock considered. "Well, the awful part is, Inspector, that I can't remember whether I did it then, or after I came out of the drawing-room. It's so much a habit. . . . I *think* I'm right in saying that I must have locked it on my way up to bed."

"It was locked when I got here; my man had to open it to me. If it was unlocked while you were talking in the drawing-room, someone could have got in from outside and gone to the telephone then."

"Well, yes, I suppose so; but who?"

"Never mind who. At least it gives me some ground-work to build upon. But supposing, for the sake of argument, that during that period when it was unlocked and you were in the drawing-room, someone came in, through here to your library and was telephoning here when you came out of the drawing-room and locked the door and went upstairs—the question then arises: How did they get out? All the other doors and windows were bolted from the *in*side; my man checked them at about eleven-fifteen. The front door is not self-locking—could anyone have let themselves out and locked it from the outside, using a key?"

"That's impossible, Inspector. I'm fussy about the keys to the front door. It hasn't got bolts or chains or anything, so we have to be careful. There are two keys, and there have never been more. I keep one and Bunsen keeps one. Last night his had been given over to your man, so for practical purposes nobody had one but myself."

"Duplicates?"

"Impossible," said Pendock again. "Mine's never been off my chain, and Bunsen is the most awful old fusspot. Anyway, why? Why should somebody have made preparations to break into my house, use my telephone, and then go away without doing anything else?" He sat up suddenly: "Good God—supposing they didn't go away—supposing they came through any old door or window that happened to be open, and simply locked and bolted it from the inside—supposing they're still in the house!"

Cockie looked at his brown fingers and smiled. "The police have these bright ideas too, Mr. Pendock. While we were in Francesca's room, my men were searching the whole place from top to bottom. No need to alarm the young ladies by saying so."

"But Fran's room—you didn't look there," cried Pendock, half-way to the door.

"Didn't I?" said Cockie coolly. As Pendock still looked anxious he added: "Fran is a blessedly untidy young woman. The doors of her cupboard were open; I

glanced into it as I left the room. There's nowhere else
in her room where anyone could hide."

Pendock felt oppressed and nervy, nevertheless.
Wearily climbing the stairs, he hoped that the little
old man was not too sanguine. Whatever happened,
he himself would stay up and watch over Fran; he
propped open the door of his bedroom, opposite hers,
and switching on his electric fire, lighted a cigarette
and sat down in a chair. . . .

Fran closed the door after Pendock's good-night,
and, still smiling, went back to her bed. The big
friendly room seemed to smile back at her in the light
of her bedside lamp; she had slept in it, on and off,
since she was a little girl, and Pendock and Bunsen
delighted to call it hers. On the painted bed was a
monogram of her initials, carved and coloured; she
plumped up the big pillow and humped the eiderdown
over her shoulders, wriggling herself into comfort with
a sigh of content. Here at least she was warm and snug
and safe, safe from the voice that had said: "Francesca's next."

The door of the cupboard began to creak.

She scrambled out of bed to shut it, thrusting her
toes into fur-lined mules that lay by the side of her bed;
and all of a sudden the room was not so friendly, the
familiar shadows were taking on strange and eerie
shapes, and all about her was a tension of something
that up to now she had hardly understood; she knew
that for the first time in her life she was afraid. She sat
rigid on the edge of the bed, clutching the eiderdown
about her with shaking hands. A white face glimmered
at her out of the gloom, and her own dark eyes stared
back at her, wide with fear, from the mirror on her
dressing-table. A woman's voice, vicious and gloating,
whispered unceasingly: "Fran's next; Francesca's
next. . . ."

Supposing that in the cupboard was crouching a
murderer—somebody not quite human, a crazy creature idly swinging to and fro that hatefully creaking
door; supposing again that the door were swinging, not

idly, but with a deadly purpose behind it—to make her do just what she was doing, to make her walk across the room to close it, into the reach of hands stretched forth to kill! In her mind she began to recite a conversation, herself very polite and reasonable, trying to explain, trying to argue, trying to temporise. . . . " 'But why should you want to kill me?' I said to her; 'I haven't done you any harm, have I?' 'No,' she said, 'you haven't done me any harm,' and she peered out of the cupboard at me, and her eyes were queer and shiny and my grey dress was hanging over her head and round her face. 'It's just that I *want* to kill,' she said, 'and you're next on my list. . . .' "

She jumped suddenly off the bed and, running across the soft carpet, pushed-to the door of the cupboard before she could give herself any more time to think. The black-lined curtains were billowing in at her wide-open window. She went to the window to shut it lest the draught from it should be swinging the cupboard door. A man's voice called up from the terrace: "Who's there? What's that?"

It made her jump, but after all it was comforting. "It's me. Francesca Hart," she called back, leaning out of the window.

Footsteps moved up the terrace; she could hear the scrunch of boots against the dry snow. "Just stay there a minute, Miss Hart, and let me see your face. Half a moment while I flash my torch."

Fears came crowding back. After all the murderer might not be a "she." Pretend for a moment that it was a man; and that the man had killed Cockie's guard out on the terrace and now was luring her to look out of the window and into the eyes of death! Supposing he should be climbing up to the sill to grasp her by the throat as she stood at the window; supposing he had a rope and flung it round her neck as she leant out, and dragged her down to the ground . . . !

There was a blinding light in her eyes, followed immediately by soft, black darkness. The voice called again: "All right, Miss. Thank you. Mustn't make any mistakes, must we? You go to bed and to sleep, Miss; I'll be watching out for you."

"Good-night," she called; and put her head out again to add: "I hope you're not terribly cold. I'm so sorry to give you all this trouble."

The window was closed and the curtains closely drawn. Somehow it was not so easy to start across the room again and get into bed. "Never again will I be superior about people who aren't brave," she vowed, and forced herself to leave the shelter of the curtains, to pass her own white ghost in the mirror and jump like a shot rabbit into the warmth and comfort and security of her bed. She sat curled up against the pillows, her shaking hands clasped against the silk and lace of her nightie, trying to still the thudding of her heart.

The curtains hung motionless now across the big window. The corners of the room were deeply shadowed in the gentle lamplight, but with shadows that she and Venetia had known from their childhood, from the days when there had been two little beds in this dear old room, when Pen and Granny had come and kissed them and tucked them up, and gone down to something grand and mysterious called Dinner that went on until the Middle of the Night. . . . She supposed that Pen had been quite young then, but he had seemed very old to them. His father had been alive, a terrifying old man whose kindly advances they had found themselves unable to welcome. . . .

She fell into a doze, still sitting curled up at the top of her bed, propped against the big white pillows. Her hands released their hold and lay with curling fingers outside the eiderdown. A soft dark curl fell over her face; she stirred and moved her head against the pillow to push it back.

Slowly the door of the cupboard began to open.

Inspector Cockrill was standing on the terrace briskly rubbing his face with his hands and stretching his aching limbs after a brief rest on Pendock's "comfortable sofa." He was paralysed by the sight of Constable Troot galloping across the grass towards him, his

mouth opening and shutting idiotically, his arms flail-
ing the innocent morning air. "They've got her, sir; the
devils . . . they've got her, sir. . . ."

"Got who? For God's sake . . ." He stumbled down
the steps and started to run across the lawn.

She was sitting in the little round summer-house
down by the railway track, propped against the
wooden wall in a strange stiff attitude, her hands hanging awkwardly at her sides; and her head had been severed from her body and sat crookedly on her mangled
neck, tied there by a bright woollen scarf. He could not
have recognised the dreadful face that leered at him,
blotchy and purple, with distended eyes; but his stomach heaved with a sort of insane relief when he saw that
the hair was not soft and dark, but a short, coarse crop
of auburn, almost like a cap. Fran was safe; but Pippi le
May was dead.

CHAPTER 5

He drew his hand across his eyes and, shuddering, looked again. Beside him, the constable stared with labouring breath, biting his finger-nail. The Inspector said at last: "Well, there it is. She's dead."

Troot wiped damp fingers on the seat of his trousers. "Yes, sir."

"We must get the doctor at once and remove that scarf; but we know what we shall find. You'd better stay here, Troot, till I send someone else along. I must go back to the house."

The summer-house was boarded in on two sides, but the rest was formed of lightly crossed branches, open to the sunshine and air. Against the boarding the snow had piled in a drift, eighteen inches deep. There were one or two half-dried puddles on the floor of the hut that might have been made by wet or snow-covered shoes, but otherwise no footprint and no sign. Around them lay the wide expanse of the lawns, sloping towards them from the house and down to the stream; and out of his childhood some memory was clamouring in the Inspector's head for recognition. He could see the dim, sexless face of his school-teacher and smell for a moment the chalky smell of the blackboard; and he was a small boy again, reciting in a gabbling monotone:

> "At Linden when the sun was low,
> All bloodless lay the untrodden snow . . ."

All bloodless. Untrodden. *Untrodden!*

A diagonal track where Troot had strolled casually down from the terrace, had suddenly quickened his pace, had stood for a moment staring and then had turned and run, stumbling, back to the house. Parallel tracks where he and Troot had come loping down together. No other mark at all. He picked his way round to the back of the little hut and looked about him: to the railway line thirty feet to the left, to the little stream fifteen feet away, and right across the drive as far as the eye could see, there was no mark at all upon the flat white surface. All bloodless lay the untrodden snow. . . . He walked slowly back to the house, examining his own tracks and those of the constable as he went.

A man was sitting quietly on a chair on the landing outside Fran's room. Cockrill called him down and spoke to him softly: "Anything to report?"

"Nothing, sir. The young lady called out in the night; her dog, sir, he'd gone to sleep in the cupboard, and he must have woke up and she saw him push open the door. Mr. Pendock came out of his room, and we both went in to the young lady and calmed her down. Nothing else at all, sir. Nobody's moved all night."

"*Have*n't they?" said Inspector Cockrill dourly, and rolled himself his first cigarette. He sent the man back to his post and went out on to the terrace below Fran's window. "Anything to report?"

"Nothing, sir. Miss Hart came to the window and shut it, and I called up and saw to it that she was all right; otherwise nothing's happened at all, sir."

"*Has*n't it?" said Cockie, and grinned quite horribly. "Well, take the car and go down at once to the village; ring up Torrington and tell them to send the doctor immediately . . . if the old man's still away, young Newsome'll have to do. And tell them to send a man to mend this bloody telephone." He stumped back into the library and, lighting the electric fire, crouched over it, rubbing his frozen hands.

Before the family was awake, the house was swarming with men. Cockrill stood among them, huddled in his great-coat, his hat sitting sideways upon his head, directing operations with vigorous sweeps of his arms;

his stubby brown fingers fumbled ceaselessly with a chain of cigarettes.

Young Dr. Newsome, so called to distinguish him from Old Dr. Newsome, his father, came into the hall; he was a tall, nice-looking boy, with his crop of curly gold hair, and beneath an air of conscious sophistication, hid an exuberant joy of living. He was highly excited by what appeared to be going to be a chain of murders at Pigeonsford, but he only said carelessly, handing over a doubtful-looking package: "Here's the scarf you wanted. I wrapped it up to keep it from messing things. The head was off all right."

"You could guess it from the way it was set. What was the weapon, do you know?"

Dr. Newsome did not know and he hated to admit it. He said, taking the cigarette out of Cockie's hand and lighting his own from it: "The head seems to be more—well, wrenched off, than cut. It's almost—" he paused with a deprecatory air—"it's almost as though two hands, two enormous hands, had seized the poor girl and twisted her head right off."

Cockie treated this statement with more respect than at first sight it appeared to deserve. He said, after a little thought: "Not the same as Miss Morland? Not the same as the girl in the wood?"

"No. Miss Morland's head was hacked off with the chopper—you can see where the blunt edges of the axe have torn the flesh; the first, of course, was cut clean off with the scythe. This is quite different; I can't tell without the P.M., naturally, but as I say, it's just as if two hands had choked the life out of the girl as they wrung off her head. . . ."

Cockie drew long and deeply on his cigarette. "We've found no weapon," he said at last, looking up at the doctor with thoughtful bright brown eyes. "Could this thing actually have been done by hands?"

"Not by human hands," said Newsome, and looked round for his instrument bag.

A sergeant came in from the garden, wiping his snowy boots on the front-door mat. "Well, sir, there's no sign of anything. We've shovelled the snow away from all around the hut and there's no weapon there; it isn't in the stream, for she's running as clear as glass; no sign of a footmark, no sign of a weapon, and no sign of blood." He shrugged his shoulders as if he, for one, gave up the puzzle.

"We'll let the household come down now, and then we can look through the bedrooms," said Cockie briefly. As the man turned away he called him back. "Bray—you're a sane sort of fellow with no funny notions, and you've had a good look at the place where the body was found. . . . Supposing the girl was murdered there, or even taken and put there after death, is it your opinion that the killer could have got away and left, as you've seen for yourself, no footprints in the snow?"

"Not on human feet," said the man, meeting the bright brown eyes.

Photographs, finger-prints, alibis . . . the family was permitted to come downstairs and was herded into the dining-room and there left in charge of a police-sergeant to drink quantities of coffee and nibble at bacon and toast. Upstairs their rooms were ransacked without success; there was no trace of blood, nothing that might conceivably have been used as a weapon, no sign that anyone had been outside the house during the previous night. Constable Wright, sniffing dreadfully, became all excited at the discovery that Pendock's shoes and overcoat were damp; but Pendock had seen Pippi home and had come back to the house through fairly heavy snow. The shoes that they had worn on their walk by the river had been drying by the kitchen fire and appeared to be undisturbed. Bunsen's coat was wet and his shoes were slightly wet, consistent with his having ridden to and from Tenfold, through the snow, on his bicycle. Otherwise clothes, shoes, everybody's possessions, all were clean and dry and free from the slightest sign of any nocturnal adventure.

Sergeant Jenkins was dispatched again for interviews with Dr. Newsome and the district nurse. Dr.

Newsome said, hopping, that Bunsen's sister was slightly better, that he believed her brother had been over to see her on the previous evening, that it was nothing to do with him anyway, and that he was in a devil of a hurry to get off on his rounds; the district nurse said that Bunsen had visited his sister again, as he had on the night of Miss Morland's death; that he had remained with her until about eleven, when he had made preparations to go, finally leaving the cottage at about ten past; and that if Sergeant Jenkins had nothing better to do than to go round asking silly questions, she *had*.

It would certainly have taken the old man, feeble and shaky as he was, an hour or nearly an hour to ride the four hilly miles through the snow; the rest of the staff, having had impregnable alibis for the time of Grace Morland's murder, might, unless one were to allow for a quite extraordinary coincidence, safely be absolved from suspicion of complicity in Pippi le May's. Inspector Cockrill, it is true, made ample allowance for coincidence, but he could find no confirmation of guilt in any of them, and they remained free from suspicion throughout the rest of the case. Bunsen also, it appeared, might be safely dismissed. Cockie, with a sigh, concentrated his attention upon the six original suspects, kept an open mind in respect of a person or persons unknown, and endeavoured to find comfort in the thought that Pippi's death did, at least, remove one potential suspect from the confusion of his investigation.

He summoned a conference in the library.

Now, indeed, terror reigned at Pigeonsford House. Pendock sought out Lady Hart. "I think you should take the girls away at once."

"I want to, Pen. Will the police let us go?"

The police most emphatically would not let them go. Cockrill, gathering the household round the library fire, spoke to them there, his face quite grey and his air of jaunty efficiency all gone. "No one must leave this house. I have sent for more men and each of you will be guarded night and day."

"I'm leaving this house at once," said Lady Hart steadily. "I'm taking my granddaughters away. You've no right to keep them here, and it isn't safe."

"You will stay here, Lady Hart, and your grand-daughters with you. I assure you they shall be safe."

"I will not stay here," cried the old lady with rising anger. "After what has happened—after this threat to Fran—I'm not going to let them stay here."

"Excuse me, Madame; you and the young ladies are staying."

"But why—*why*?" she cried, all her anger and defiance breaking down against the wall of his stony determination. "Why should you keep them here? For God's sake let me take them away from this place, or let them go alone—but let them go. Dear Cockie, let them go! Why must you keep them here?"

He did not answer her or meet her tearful eyes, but he undid a package that he held loosely wrapped up in his hand and took out a woollen scarf. "Have any of you seen this before?"

"It's Pippi's," said Venetia, leaning forward to look at it. She added suddenly, and her voice went weak with horror: "It's all over blood!"

Fran put her hand to her mouth: "Oh, God, I feel sick. . . ."

"Yes, it's all over blood," said Cockrill calmly, folding it up and replacing it in its paper. "Now—each of you in turn: when did you see it last?"

They had seen it when Pippi came up to dinner the night before, wrapped round her head and tucked about her throat; and again when she had put it on to go home through the snow. "After that she lent it to my housemaid to come back in," said Pendock, shuddering away from the parcel in the Inspector's hand. "I took it from the girl in the hall and put it in a drawer. I meant to give it back to Miss le May to-day."

"Who knew you had put it in the drawer?"

"Well, everybody knew," said Pendock doubtfully.

"Mr. Pendock came in and told us," said Henry from the arm of Venetia's chair. "He said he had put it in the little drawer in the hall-stand, and if any of us saw her next day—to-day that is—would we see that she got it back."

"You all heard him say this?"

They had all heard. "What about the maid, Mr. Pendock? Did you tell the maid?"

Gladys was sent for and arrived in the safe conduct of Constable Wright, but was so genuinely shaken by the whole dreadful affair that she forbore to make any exhibition of herself. She replied in a subdued voice that the master had told her to hand the scarf over to him, and that she had then left the hall and had no idea what had happened to it. "Innercent Girl questioned by Brutal Police," thought Gladys drearily, scurrying back to the kitchen.

"What else was kept in this drawer?" said Cockie, when she had gone.

"As it happens there was nothing else in it."

"Were there any other scarves on the stand?"

"Two or three," said Pendock indifferently.

"So you see." He fixed them with those beady brown eyes that now seemed inimical to them all. "The girl's scarf was in a certain drawer. Six of you knew where it was. Her murderer ignored all the other scarves on the hall-stand, went to the drawer where her own scarf had been put, took that out, and used it to—well, he used it. Why he took it—we don't know. Who took it—we don't know. But only six people had the knowledge that that scarf was in that drawer. Now, Lady Hart, you can see why three of those people are not to be given permission to leave this house."

She struggled to her feet, angry again, and frightened and bewildered. "Surely you don't think that one of these girls—one of these young girls . . ."

"How should I know?" said Cockie, shrugging his shoulders.

"I should think you would only have to look at them," said James suddenly, opening his sleepy brown eyes and looking at them himself.

The Inspector looked too, and very pretty and fresh and sweet they were. "Supposing we let them go," he said to James, "because they are such particularly

charming creatures. Who shall we send with them?
Are we to suppose that they won't be safe with their
grandmother?—of course not. So she goes too. But
then, Mrs. Gold's legal guardian is her husband, and
will she allow us to suggest that she would be in danger
from him? Oh no! So that leaves yourself and Mr. Pendock. But I have known Mr. Pendock for years, and
respected him and liked him for years. So that leaves
you. With your help, Captain Nicholl, we are working
pretty fast. I'd better let you all go and start combing
the countryside for a convenient tramp."

"Ah, yes, what about the tramp?" cried Fran eagerly, trotting off after this timely hare. "Was it him
that killed poor Miss Morland?"

Cockie raised a cynical eyebrow. "What do you
think?"

"*I* d'know," she said, abashed. "Didn't he? You said
he'd confessed; you thought yourself, last night, that it
was him."

Cockie ignored this hardy thrust. He said instead:
"Apart from the butler, only six of you knew about
Francesca's hat; only six of you knew about the le May
girl's scarf. And last night, while Miss le May was
being murdered, the 'tramp' was safely locked up in
the Torrington gaol."

Pendock was standing with his back to the fire, rocking gently from his toes to his heels with a monotonous
regularity. "Pen, for God's sake stand still!" cried Lady
Hart. She added immediately: "I'm sorry, darling; my
nerves have all gone phut."

He sat on the arm of her chair and took her plump
hand in his. "Don't be too worried; it'll all be all right."
And to Cockrill he suggested coolly: "Perhaps you
could explain how any of these dear people could have
killed Miss le May? At just before eleven I saw her
home; till after half-past eleven they were all together
playing Vingt-et-un in the drawing-room; from midnight onwards your men were all over the place. That
leaves less than half an hour in which any of them
could have got the girl out of her house; done what

was—done; come back here for the scarf, tied her up in it and got themselves to bed."

"We can cut quite a few minutes out of that programme by supposing that the murderer took the scarf with him when he came out of this house," suggested Cockie.

"He never came out of this house," cried Pendock angrily.

"Then how did he know where you had put the scarf?"

He turned his head from side to side, away from the horrible truth. "God knows—*I* don't."

"Don't you? And yet you're the most likely person to know, Mr. Pendock, aren't you?" said Cockie swiftly. "In your premises just now you skirted rather lightly over the fact that *you* weren't playing Vingt-et-un in the drawing-room. *You* would have had more than twenty minutes, Mr. Pendock, to do 'what was done' and tie the girl up in the scarf—wouldn't you?"

"He didn't skirt over it at all," cried Fran passionately. "He wasn't talking about himself; he was only thinking of us. Of course he didn't do it—of *course* Pen didn't do it."

"How do you know?" said Cockie, with patient sarcasm.

"Because of the telephone call," cried Fran triumphantly. "What about that? You'd forgotten about that, hadn't you? But it was definitely made, or at any rate started, while Pen was talking to us in the drawing-room. Now who made that call? There *was* somebody else in the house who might be the murderer. Pen couldn't have made the call."

The old man nodded his head at her and grinned. "All right, young lady. Well done." He looked round at their hostile faces and perceived that in his own fear and anxiety he was alienating their sympathy with him. "Now, don't let's quarrel," he said pacifically. "We want to help each other; I'm here to help you. If the murderer isn't one of your number, well, of course, we must find him; if he *is* one of you, we must find him just the same—mustn't we? Come on, let's have a

talk. . . . I want you to give me some help." He drew
up a chair to the fire and sat down, leaning forward
with a confidential air. "This Pippi le May—she was an
actress, wasn't she?"

"Yes," said Pendock, somewhat mollified.

"She came down here frequently in the summer?"

"Yes. She had for years. To tell you the truth, I think
she reckoned it was a cheap holiday."

"Miss Morland didn't leave her anything that would
now pass on to her next of kin, do you know?"

"She left her a pinchbeck bracelet and a painting of
the Church Tower in Blossom Time," said James, without enthusiasm.

Cockrill looked surprised. "You seem very well informed in the matter."

"She told Pendock and myself yesterday afternoon
as we were walking along the river bank," said James.

"I see. Now you all knew her pretty well, I take it?"

"We met her almost every summer when we stayed
here with Mr. Pendock," said Lady Hart. "The young
people used to bathe together and have picnics and so
on. We knew her as well as that, but no better. Not
intimately."

"And Mr. Gold? You were not a member of the family in those days."

"I never met her till last summer," said Henry. "We
spent the last week of our honeymoon here, Venetia
and I, and I said 'How d'you do' to Pippi half a dozen
times, and that was all. And of course I saw her yesterday."

"And once in London," said Venetia.

"Oh yes, if that counts. I met her one day in a tube,
and walked as far as the theatre with her, and she
promised to send me complimentary tickets for her
show and never did."

Pendock smiled. "She promised me complimentary
tickets for her show with unfailing regularity for twelve
or fifteen years, but I've never had one yet. I suppose
she did it to everyone."

"Yes, she did," said James.

They all looked round at him, puzzled at the tone of his voice. "She promised tickets to you also, did she?" said Cockie, narrowing his little eyes.

James threw a coin into the air and caught it neatly. "Yes, she did. And what's more she sent them, too."

Cockie was not fond of James; he was irritated by his expressionless face and air of lazy calm, and by the knowledge that James could withdraw into some world of his own, and remain immune from blustering authority. He said nastily: "And how do you account for that? Why did she get them for you when she let other people down?"

"I suppose because she was my wife," said James, and tossed his coin and neatly caught it again.

Cockrill was too much astonished, himself, to observe that, in the expressions of at least two of those present, surprise was absent. His first reaction was a slightly embarrassed review of the things he might have said about Pippi in James's hearing. When this very human aspect had been dealt with, however, he was sufficiently in command of himself to request immediate silence and to instruct Constable Wright to take the party, excluding James, to the drawing-room; to remain there with them and to see that nobody spoke a word to anyone else. "I shall ask you, one by one, what you know about this," said Cockie, quite dropping his air of friendly conspiracy, and he rubbed his thin hands together and thought: "A motive at last!"

They filed out of the room, Pendock very grave and anxious, Henry and Venetia bewildered, Fran looking back at James with a troubled face; but at the door Lady Hart swung suddenly and cried to the Inspector in a strangled, shaking voice: "Don't think *I* knew anything about this! *I* knew nothing about it!" and turned upon Fran stricken and beseeching eyes. The constable put his hand on her arm and shut the door in her face.

A man followed Fran and Venetia on to the terrace and across the snow-covered lawn. In the far corner made by the intersection of the stream and the railway line the dark little hump of the summer-house was surrounded by small black figures that stood and jerked and ran about their mysterious duties. The sound of their voices carried sharply in the cold, clear air; the summer-house, which in the ordinary way one never noticed at all, seemed to obtrude its presence all over the grounds. Fran said distressfully: "Can't we get out of the garden and go somewhere else? I can't stick it here."

"We could ask the man, I suppose."

"I wouldn't dare," said Fran listlessly.

Venetia would dare anything for anyone she loved. She turned to the policeman behind them and said in her sweet, cool voice: "Could we possibly go for a walk, just over the fields? We could cross the railway line and go along the stream—do you think we might? It's not very nice here . . ." She nodded vaguely in the direction of the summer-house.

The stream ran between two innocent fields. "I think you might go there, Miss," said the constable kindly. "I'll have to come along with you, and of course you mustn't go far. . . ." He stood looking down at them, a thick-set, powerful man; he was not one to imagine things, but really they put you in mind of the pictures of them refugees, with their pale faces and sorrowful eyes, and three-cornered scarves tied under their chins. "I'll walk along be'ind you, Miss," he said to Venetia.

They crossed the railway line, scrunching through the snow that lay piled against its banks, and cut across the field to where they had walked by the stream the day before. They did not touch each other, but they were very near in spirit with the curious kinship of the twin born. Fran said, speaking softly, so that their guardian might not hear: "I'm nearly frantic, darling; I've been pining all day to talk to you."

"It's all been so dreadful, Fran. Miss Morland, here, in the garden . . . you just can't believe it, can you? And Pippi; killed like that, Fran, here at Pigeonsford. . . . I mean, we knew her so *well*. And oh, dar-

ling, what *is* all this about James? I can't believe that
he of all people—I'd have sworn that he was the most
honest and truthful person one could possibly know; I
can't believe that he would make love to you and everything and all the time be married . . . and to Pippi le
May. . . ."

"But darling, he *didn't*. I mean, I knew. He told me
that night in the orchard, and of course he was going to
arrange about a divorce."

"Oh, Fran, you might have told *me*."

"I was going to, Venetia, naturally; but the very next
morning poor Miss Morland was killed and I didn't get
a chance, and then I suddenly thought of something
and I began to worry like hell. You know the night before Miss Morland had told Trotty that she had somebody in the 'hollow of her hand'? well—" she looked
apologetic—"it seems very dramatic and silly, but I
thought she might have meant James; I didn't know
what to do, Venetia, I was worried to death. I thought
the police would be asking questions and the fewer
people who knew about James being married to Pippi,
the better. Your face always gives you away, darling;
you simply can't tell lies. And we might have had to tell
some lies."

"I can't make head or tail of what you're talking
about, Fran," said Venetia. "Begin at the beginning,
for goodness' sake, and tell me all about it. If there are
any lies to be told, I'll tell them for you all right." She
added deliberately: "And for James too, if he needs
them."

Fran smiled at her, and for no reason her eyes were
suddenly filled with tears. "Thank you, sweetie; it was
nice of you to say that. I don't think he will need them
now, but I'm glad you feel that way about him."

"But tell me about Pippi," said Venetia.

"Oh yes, Pippi. Well, you see, we knew James was
keen on me, didn't we? But only because it sort of
stood out a mile, not from anything he said, because he
never did say anything. In other words he wasn't going
to ask me to marry him until he'd settled about a divorce and all that. Then that afternoon that Miss Mor-

land was here to tea, Pen rather showed his hand; and
James was afraid I might say yes to Pen before I knew
that he, James, was in the running—which, as a matter
of fact, after your lecture about not waiting to fall
madly in love with someone, I might have. He asked
me to meet him that evening and talk to him, and he
was going to tell me then; but during dinner Pippi rang
up from Torrington station and said that she was going
to the cottage and that she wanted to see him. . . ."

"How did she know he was here?"

"Well, *I* don't know, darling—she rang up the mess
or something, I suppose—anyway, he met her in the
orchard at about ten o'clock; he couldn't meet her in
the house, because of course Miss Morland didn't
know they were married."

"But when were they married, Fran? Why didn't we
know? Why didn't they tell us?"

"Oh yes, I forgot that. Well, he married her ages ago,
when they were both about twenty or something. They
had met each other a lot down here in the summer holidays, when we still hardly knew either of them, and
they got very thick, sailing and so forth. I should think,
knowing Pippi, that she led poor James up the garden a
bit, because if he's a bit of a goof now, it's nothing to
what he was then; anyway, he went on seeing her in
London, after one particular summer, and finally they
got married. James was up at Cambridge and Pippi was
on tour in some show or other, so they didn't live together or have a home or anything; and what was more
important, they were terrified of James's uncle finding
out. You know the old boy was terribly straitlaced, and
the bare fact that Pippi was an actress would have sent
him up in blue smoke apparently, and of course he was
all for James waiting till he was about forty and a pillar
of the Firm, and then marrying somebody pretty
worthy—I mean a mayor's daughter or something like
that; so they kept it all a deathly secret and James just
sent Pippi money out of his allowance, which was a
pretty hearty one, and they saw each other now and
again when they were both in London, and by the end
of a year or so they were both already sick of the whole

affair. Pippi had kept her stage name, of course, and nobody knew that James was married; they decided they'd go on like that till either of them actually wanted to be free. It seemed a good idea to James, poor innocent, because of course a divorce would have packed him up completely with his uncle; and as for Pippi— well, she's dead and all that, but one can't help saying that she knew that one day James would come in for a lot of money, if she could spin it out (being paid pretty comfortably for nothing, in the meantime) till the old boy died. Anyway, they just saw each other occasionally, but only as 'brother and sister' as the papers say; and then James began to fall for me."

"Well, I'm glad it was only that. I mean only a 'boy and girl romance,' again as the papers say, and not a whole history of loving and living together and having a home and so forth, before James fell in love with you."

"Ah, but you're more romantic than me, Venetia," said Fran, laughing.

Venetia laughed too. "I expect you're quite glad yourself, in spite of being so hard-boiled."

"Yes, I am, quite. Anyway, the thing is that Pippi, the day before she came down here, had seen in the papers that James's uncle had died and duly left him the packet; and on the strength of it she'd turned down her own boy friend, who's been going for years, and had come down to tell James that she could do with a few more conjugal rights. And James meets her with the information that he wants a divorce to marry somebody else!"

"Oh, heavens, Fran, what a muddle. And how very—I mean, it *is* rather sordid, darling."

"Yes, I know, but it can't be helped. After all, it wasn't poor James that made it sordid; he was terribly upset about it, but having arranged with me to come out to the orchard, he couldn't just say nothing, so he told me all about it, and asked me if I would marry him if he did manage to get the divorce. By that time he'd started telling me, so he had to go on, and stop being

the little gentleman and never disclosing his true feelings."

"But how did you get out of the house?" said Venetia, her mind on more practical matters than the ethics
of James's proposal. "I thought the front door was
locked, and you can't unlock it, even from the inside,
without the key."

"Yes, it was locked. It was a bit of a shock to me
when I realised that, because James was already out in
the orchard, waiting for me . . . actually, he was talking to Pippi, but of course I didn't know that; and he'd
made the date with me before she rang him up. Of
course I told Pen he was in bed. You see, knowing how
Pen felt, I didn't want to upset him by being seen in a
huddle with James, especially if nothing was going to
come of it, and at that time I didn't know if anything
was: in fact I still don't. But if Pen was going to be in
love with me, it was only fair to hear James's side too,
wasn't it?"

"Well, but how did you get out, Fran? You tell a
story in the most muddled way I ever heard in my life."

"It's you asking questions that muddles it. Where
was I? Oh yes, at the front door. Well, it wouldn't open,
so I went to the back door; that has a Yale, and it
wasn't bolted because Bunsen was out at Tenfold. I
went out that way and left the latch fastened back so
that we could get in again; when we came back we simply clicked the door to, and it was just as I found it."

"But *Fran*—that means that anyone could have got
into the house and taken your hat from the hall!"

"But no one could have known that the back door
would be open for that ten minutes or so; and as it was,
it didn't matter if they did, because the box was still
quite all right when we came back through the hall.
Don't agitate: I've told Cockie all about it. Anyway, I
went down to the orchard and there was James, and he
was so sweet and it was so lovely!"

"I'm sure it was," said Venetia, laughing at her.

"No, but honestly. There was the most marvellous
moon, and the trees looked all silver and the downs

were white and the stream gurgling away under the bridge. . . . Pigeonsford looked like a big black mass standing up across the lawn. . . ." She added, laughing: "And it was terribly cold!"

They came to the end of the field. Their bodyguard joined them for a moment. "If you don't mind, Miss, I think you'd better turn back here; you can turn again at the other end if you want to, but the Inspector wouldn't like it if I let you go further from the house than this."

They turned obediently. "So we decided to go in," said Fran from where she had left off. "We thought that now everyone was in bed we could sit in the library and talk it over by the fire. So that's what we did."

"What time was that, Fran?"

"Very soon after eleven. We came up to the house and went into the library and shut the door and sat over the fire and talked, and James kissed me a good deal. He was awfully sweet, no funny business or anything like that. He *is* nice, Venetia."

"How long were you in the library with James kissing you a good deal and no funny business?"

"Oh, hours. Of course we were talking, and James was telling me about Pippi, and I was trying to discuss with him whether it would be a good idea for me to marry him; but he was rather one-sided about that."

Venetia laughed again. "You *are* a funny child, Fran. Fancy asking poor James to make up your mind for you! Don't you know it yourself?"

"Well, I feel as if I do, Venetia. At least I feel very sloppy about James and I like being kissed by him and at first I minded quite a lot about his having been married to Pippi; but I've felt like that about a lot of other people—I couldn't be certain if it was the genuine article, in fact I don't see how one can tell. You said yourself earlier that afternoon to choose somebody to marry that I didn't love too painfully, like you love Henry, so I was trying to make out if James would like to marry me under those terms . . . I mean if I turned out to be not wildly in love with him. . . ."

"I see," said Venetia, still smiling.

"Anyway, we sat there talking it over, and imagine our horror when we heard voices outside and somebody seemed to be saying something to Granny, calling up to her window; and then feet came running downstairs and through the hall and out of the front door. We couldn't think what was the matter unless it was a warden about the lights showing; but, anyway, we thought we'd better hop upstairs and go to bed as if we'd been there all night. So we did. I scrambled out of my clothes and got into bed, and when Granny and Pen came in I pretended to be sound asleep; they never dreamt that I hadn't been there all night," said Fran innocently. "James says he actually fell asleep, but of course he was even quicker into bed than I was."

"I noticed you hadn't taken off your make-up," said Venetia. "I was going to tell you about it and say you'd ruin your skin."

"Did you notice it? So did Cockie, the old devil. We thought we'd better explain to him, in case he found out for himself and thought there was more in it than there really was; but I asked him not to tell Granny or anybody, as there didn't seem to be any point, and she would have thought it dreadful for me to be sitting up all alone with James. Funny thing," said Fran, as so many of her generation have said before her, "that elderly people never will believe that anyone can remain moral after eleven o'clock at night."

"But the man Pippi saw in the orchard—don't you remember? She said she was walking there about half-past ten and she saw a man—why, Fran, she must have been with James then."

"Yes, of course she was. He was the only man she ever saw in the orchard. You see, after Grace Morland was found, there wasn't an opportunity for them to talk to each other and discuss what they were going to tell and what they weren't going to tell. So when we were all having breakfast that morning, and Pippi came in—you remember?—James said to her: 'What were you doing last night at half-past ten?' meaning what have you told the *police* you were doing, and Pippi saw what he meant immediately, and said that she'd told

them she was alone; and just in case they should know
there'd been someone else in the orchard at that time,
or in case James should want to say he'd been there
too, she made up a story about having seen a man
strolling there, though she didn't know who it was. It
was jolly quick of her, wasn't it?"

"I don't see why she didn't tell the truth straight
out."

"I should think it was because of Grace Morland's
peculiar remark about the hollow of her hand," said
Fran doubtfully. "Trotty must have told Pippi in the
morning after Grace Morland was found dead, though
of course *we* didn't know about it till later on. Pippi
thought Grace must have seen her and James from her
bedroom window—you know how the orchard comes
right up under the side windows of Pigeonsford Cottage. She thought James might be involved in some
way, so she played for safety by not saying anything to
the police. Then yesterday afternoon she got rid of Pen
while he was walking with her and James by the river,
and they talked the whole thing over; and after we
came back from the walk James told me, and we all
three went to Cockie—in easy stages of course, not
together—and told him exactly what had happened.
The only thing we didn't say was that Pippi was married to James; we thought we could just tell him later
on if it began to matter—it didn't seem to have anything to do with Grace. Of course, now that poor
Pippi's dead, it had to come out."

They crossed over the railway line and back into
Pigeonsford grounds. "I'm afraid it's been a terrible
shock to Gran."

Fran walked beside her sister with bent head, her
hands in their big fur gloves linked behind her back.
She did not reply.

"Gran's so frightfully against divorce and things like
that," went on Venetia, pursuing her own train of
thought. "I'm afraid she'd have been awfully upset in
any case; I don't think she'd have liked you to have
married James, you know, if she'd known he'd been
married already."

"She did know," said Fran in a muffled voice.

Venetia stood stock still, looking at her twin with wide-open, startled eyes. "You'd told her?"

"Yes. I told her yesterday, when we were walking by the river. I got her to say that she thought James was the right man for me to marry and all that, and then, when I knew what she really thought of him as a person, I told her about his being married to Pippi, and asked if she'd mind me marrying him if he was divorced. She was frightfully upset and said it was absolutely impossible; especially as Pippi looked like making a fuss and not letting him go too easily now that he's come in for his money."

"You told her yesterday?"

"Yes," said Fran, not meeting her sister's eyes.

But that morning she had turned at the door of the library and cried out to Cockie that *she* knew nothing about James's marriage; had looked at Fran as though to beg her to keep quiet. . . .

"Wasn't it *peculiar*," said Fran in a sad, small voice.

Pendock sought out the Inspector. "Look here, Cockrill, I'm going to ask you a favour. If I stay in this house a moment longer I shall go off my head. I've always walked a lot and I simply must get some exercise. Couldn't you let me go out on the downs and stretch my legs a bit?"

"No," said Cockie crossly, for he had been interrupted in the middle of a most elaborate timetable.

"Oh, but Cockrill—look. I feel absolutely stifled here. Do let me go. . . ."

"What do you want to go for?" said Cockie irritably.

"I tell you, I want to walk. That's all. I won't stop anywhere or speak to anyone, I won't do anything but simply walk. Couldn't you let me go?"

"I could let you go with a guard, I suppose," said the Inspector ungraciously.

"Oh, God, that's no good. It's the very feeling of being guarded, cramped up mentally and physically, that I want to get away from." He turned like a caged animal, wounded and desperate, driven by something more than the mere desire of an hour or two of exercise. "Well—all right," he said hopelessly.

Cockie raised his bright little eyes and looked him in the face. "Mr. Pendock—you are under at least some suspicion for the murders of Grace Morland and Miss le May. How am I to know that you aren't planning some kind of a get-away?"

Pendock looked horrified. "*I'm* under suspicion?"

"Of course. You're all under suspicion."

"But, Inspector, I was in bed. . . ."

"I know, I know, I know," said Cockie wearily. "You are all as innocent as the babe unborn and the two unfortunate ladies murdered each other and replaced their own heads by post-mortem muscular contraction. I know." He pointed suddenly across the village to where the downs rolled out above and beyond. "Now look here—from this house I shall be able to watch you if you walk to the Tenfold Ridge and down again. You ought to be through the village and out of the valley in a quarter of an hour; and from then on I shall keep you in sight." He interrupted Pendock's gratitude to add: "But you must have someone with you. Captain Nicholl had better go."

Pendock's face fell. "He won't walk a yard if he can help it."

"Well, what about Mr. Gold?"

"He'd come. I expect he'd love it. But wouldn't either of them help me in my dash for liberty?"

"That's my business," said Cockie briefly. He took out his watch. "You must be back in two hours. And no nonsense: straight up to the ridge and down again. I shall have a squint through glasses now and again, so don't try bribing any of your local adherents to understudy you."

Henry was delighted to go. They collected Aziz and set off through the village among the doubtful glances of many whom Pendock had befriended in other days, now all quite ready to throw stones if stones were put into their hands. The evacuees had not been so thrilled since a bomb had fallen two doors away, at home in dear old Whitechapel. They asked eagerly of Pendock's tenants: "Is it true that 'is father done in 'is mother?" and the villagers who had waxed fat and comfortable and happy under generations of Pendocks replied regretfully that it was not strictly true; though the lady had died very young and there might be something in that. "And what's more she died abroad," added Mrs. Porter, the green-grocer's wife, leaning across the counter with rather special care because she was shortly expecting her sixth.

A rustle of excitement passed among the evacuees. They said darkly: "Wot—at Ostend or somethink of that?"

Mrs. Porter did not think that Mrs. Pendock had died at Ostend. "Well, never mind—as long as it was abroad," said the evacuees cheerfully, for who knew what dark things might not go on abroad, what with them casinos and things; and here was this grand-looking gentleman right in their midst, right in this dead-and-alive little village where people drank their milk straight from the cow and not out of nice hygienic tins, and only the ladies of the gentry went into the pub; here he was follering in his father's footsteps and who knew where it would end? They gazed after him with respectful horror.

Pendock was unmoved. "People are all the same. This very same lot will fall over themselves to rejoice with me when the whole thing's cleared up and 'the House' is free from suspicion. I don't care two hoots what they think."

"Don't you?" said Henry, picking up this brave challenge as he did everything that could be of interest or present a new point of view. "You're a very lucky man if you don't. Personally I feel as though tadpoles were wriggling up and down my spine, and after all *I* don't know them—they're nothing to me. Do you really not mind?"

"Why should I? It's only instinct, not reason. They're nice people, really; I don't know much about the evacuees, of course, though I saw a lot of them when they first came and I was fixing up for their reception and so on; but the villagers are good, simple, straightforward folk. It's just that they're sheep—like the vast majority of the human race. Why should I be hurt by what they think? Anyway, it'll all be cleared up in a day or two. . . ."

"Do you think so?" said Henry gravely. "Myself, I'm not so sure. To me it all looks very queer and ugly and very frightening indeed."

They turned out of the village and began to climb the gentle ascent to the downs. Aziz ran before them with the busy, important look that Fran called "swinging his brief-case." Pendock said slowly: "It's queer, of course; and ugly, of course; but what is there to be frightened of? We're safe enough, really."

"Do you think we are?" said Henry coolly.

"Well, we've got the police guard."

"The police guard didn't help Pippi," said Henry sombrely. "Anyway, I didn't mean that sort of danger. I meant that sooner or later Cockrill is going to pick on one of us and clap us into gaol. He wouldn't be human if he didn't; after all he's got to have something to show for three decapitations."

As they climbed the hill out of the village Pendock's mind began to swing round to confidence. He said reasonably: "He couldn't do it. There's another person mixed up in all this who hasn't appeared yet, and once they turn up we'll have nothing to worry about. I grant you it's odd about the hat and again about the scarf; but we were all together when that 'phone call was made, and that's the beginning and end of it. There must be someone else."

"But how did that person get out of the house, Pendock? That's what hasn't been explained. She was telephoning when you came out of the drawing-room; we've established the time sufficiently to prove that she was either still on the 'phone or else that she'd just finished the call. As you didn't see her in the hall she must have been in the library. On your way upstairs you locked the front door; well, how did she get out?"

"Back door," suggested Pendock doubtfully.

"The only way you can get to the back door is through the servants' hall and the kitchen, and Constable Whatsit was drinking coffee in there with the rest of the staff. Anyway, the back door, like everything else in the house, was found locked and bolted on the *in*side."

"That applies to us too," said Pendock. "I could have got in and out because I've got a key to the front door, only as it happens, I didn't. But none of *you* could."

It was like coming out of a fog, to be striding over the downs in the cold crisp air, with the world all white about them; he felt as though he had been stifled down in Pigeonsford, stifled in doubts and suspicions and vague, uneasy fears. Here he could breathe freely and think clearly and without small prejudices. For the first time he faced with courage the thought of the threat to Fran: he took it in his hands and broke it apart and examined it, and much of his terror and foreboding crumbled with it. "After all, Fran *wasn't* next," he said aloud. "It was all just an empty threat to draw attention from Pippi le May. I believe, I do believe, that the whole thing has been directed against Miss Morland's family; somebody wanted to wipe them out and they used all these tricks to try and involve us at Pigeonsford. . . ."

"But what about the girl in the copse? She wasn't connected with Miss Morland."

"Oh, the girl in the copse had nothing to do with it," said Pendock, swinging his stick almost light-heartedly, trudging along through the snow. "Somebody wanted to do away with Miss Morland and her cousin; the business in the summer had never been explained, so they thought they would confuse the issue by committing the murder in a rather similar way. I don't believe there's any other connection."

"I got rather confidential with my bodyguard this morning," said Henry, who could draw confidences from a boa-constrictor. "Apparently there were some very odd points about Miss le May's murder. Did you know, for example, that the body was surrounded by acres of snow, untrodden by human foot?"

"Good lord—is that so?"

"And moreover, the police have turned the house up-side down, as we've very good cause to know, and they haven't found a weapon. My chum firmly believes that Pippi le May murdered Grace Morland and that Grace has come back with a chopper from the other world, and done the same for Pippi. The police seem to think that she may have been killed somewhere else and then dumped in the summer-house; but, either way, she had to be got there, and the other person had to get away. How the devil was it done?"

"Parachute!" suggested Pendock, smiling, watching Aziz as he tunnelled his way through the snow, his tail moving like a small black periscope against the white surface.

"A parachute isn't much good at taking off again," said Henry, responding to his smile. His eager mind toyed lovingly with the problem. "I suggested tennis rackets tied over the shoes and of course skis and all the winter sports dodges; but my man says there just weren't any marks at all. Fascinating, isn't it?"

"It might be, if it hadn't happened in my garden," said Pendock ruefully.

"I thought somebody might have got away by the railway line," continued Henry cheerfully. "Walking along balancing on the rails, you know. That wouldn't leave any prints. But apart from the fact that it's diffi-cult to do a tight-rope act along slippery rails at the best of times, and rather more so when you're encum-bered by a headless body—or any other kind of body, for the matter of that—it would still leave a distance of fifteen to twenty yards to be covered between the rail-way line and the summer-house." He stopped sud-denly, and his face was alive with a sort of mischievous enlightenment. "I say! Didn't you tell me that Grace Morland's maid had been a tight-rope walker?"

For a moment the sheer coincidence was almost too much for Pendock; but he laughed and pushed aside the whole idea. "She can hardly walk along the ground these days, poor old Trotty, let alone a tight-rope; and anyway, she was a trapeze artist, not a wire-walker. Besides which she's old and feeble and everything else

you can think of. Be*sides* which she owed an awful lot
to the Morland family, and now that Grace is dead,
loses a good home and a comfortable job and has only
a pittance to live on in place of it."

"For all you know she loathed the family like poi-
son," insisted Henry, reluctant to abandon his brilliant
brain-wave, though he did not for a moment really believe in it. "For all you know, her legs are as strong as
yours or mine. Who says she's a cripple? Trotty says
so; no one else."

"An eminent specialist from London said so some
years ago," said Pendock, laughing at him. "And various doctors and nurses and masseurs at Torrington
Cottage Hospital say so to this day; otherwise I must
admit that her claims are quite unsubstantiated."

"Well, I'm sorry about it," said Henry. He added
apologetically: "It's a shame to joke about it; but up
here everything seems very remote and unimportant,
doesn't it?"

They had reached the crest of the downs and now
leant, puffing, against a boulder, looking down on the
rolling, snow-covered grassland stretching out ahead of
them; and back to where Pigeonsford stood out, big
and black and square, on the rising ground the other
side of the valley. Henry Gold, who all his life had been
a Londoner, knew for the first time that strange sense
of proportion that comes of watching, from a lonely
height, the little works of man. He looked down upon
the small black ants toiling in the valley, and knew that
he was God; he looked up at the glazed white bowl of
the winter sky, and knew that he was the least of the
little ants, scurrying this way and that in futile endeav-
our to avoid extinction by the careless feet of time; it
frightened him a little, but he felt cleansed and chas-
tened by the loneliness and silence. He looked at Pendock leaning quietly against the rock beside him, and
felt easier with him, more genuinely loyal towards him,
than he had for many hours past. He realised that in all
the horror of these dreadful two days, his values had
slipped a little, and that though he had not for a moment consciously suspected his friends, his mind had

retreated into a sort of reticence, a sort of unformulated doubt. Now he could see so clearly that some person was involved in the murders other than the six of them, and all the uneasiness was banished from his mind. It seemed that Pendock had undergone a similar purification for he said, smiling, as they started back down the hill: "There's nothing like heights, even a gentle height like this, to bring one back to one's senses. I didn't realise it before, but do you know I was almost suspecting *you*!"

"I was definitely suspecting you," said Henry, smiling back at him. "Of course I didn't realise it either, but as you say, being up on a hill and out of the world pulls you together a bit. I do see now that there must have been somebody else; if only because otherwise it would *have* to be you!"

They both thought this an excellent joke. "But how do you make it out, anyway?"

"Well, unless we subscribe to my bodyguard's theory of post-mortem revenge on the part of Miss Morland, it couldn't be anyone else, could it? I mean, we don't seriously suppose that somebody put poor Pippi's body in the summer-house and marched off, whistling, leaving no footprints where he trod. He left footprints like anybody else. But the footprints were covered up. By snow, of course."

"In other words the thing was done before the snow stopped falling?"

"Yes, exactly. And it stopped snowing at midnight. Pippi was seen alive at eleven, so that leaves an hour. For about forty minutes of that hour, Lady Hart and Fran and Venetia and James and I were together in the drawing-room, and saying good-night on the stairs; besides, the house was locked up and I really don't see how any of us could have got out or in. But you could, old boy. You had the key. And what's more, you had a whole hour."

"Thanks very much," said Pendock, liking it a trifle less. "What am I supposed to have done with my hour?"

"This is only what I was thinking," said Henry hastily. "At least, I wasn't even thinking it, but it was at the back of my mind. Because of course you *could* have got out and done the girl in and dumped her in the summerhouse, and been back in bed by the time we all came upstairs." He glanced at Pendock with his disarming smile.

"What did I do with the weapons?" said Pendock coldly.

"Don't take this the wrong way, Pen," said Henry, venturing upon the shortened form of his name for the first time in their acquaintance. "We were only saying what we had in our minds before the cobwebs got blown away. I mean, it was obviously the only solution, unless there was some unknown person involved. We've agreed that there *was* someone else in the house; someone was telephoning in the library when you went upstairs."

"But they couldn't have got out," said Pendock irritably. "You said so yourself, half an hour ago. And how did they know Miss Morland had said that she wouldn't be seen dead in Fran's hat? And what about Pippi's scarf? No one could have known it was in that drawer—except us six. . . ."

The village closed about them. As they turned in to its little main street Pendock was thinking that "in the back of his mind" Henry had been entertaining some remarkably well-formulated theories against himself; walking past the pub, Henry told himself that, dash it all, he hardly knew the fellow, had never set eyes on him until last year, though he had heard so much about him from Venetia; turning in at the gates of Pigeonsford House, it occurred to them both that James, though they had thought they knew him so well, had proved to be a bit of a mystery, marrying that frightful le May girl behind all their backs; and as they trudged up the drive, cross and out of sorts, they remembered what an imperious, self-willed woman was Lady Hart. Pendock thought of Venetia, docile and gentle, and easily led by those she loved, doting on this wretched little Jew;

Henry thought of Fran, petted, high-tempered, way-ward, resolute; and as they mounted the steps to the big front door, the network of uneasy suspicion was about them once again. The gods had come back to the ant-heap and were making themselves at home.

Lady Hart and James asked for no favours but walked up and down the terrace, side by side. James muttered something under his breath. "What did you say?" asked Lady Hart sharply.

"Did I say something?" said James, mildly astonished. "I'm sorry. I was thinking about the snow; I must have been quoting."

"Well, don't quote," said Lady Hart irritably, for she had brought James out to tell him what she thought of him, and this was not the beginning she had prepared. "And there are rather more important things to be thought about than the snow."

"The police don't seem to agree with you," suggested James, pointing to where the constabulary of Torrington revolved uneasily about the summer-house. "They've measured the distance between the railway and the summer-house fourteen times, to my certain knowledge."

"You're playing for time, James," said Lady Hart severely and, as it happened, unjustly. "I came out here to say something to you, and it was this: I think you have been very cruel to Fran and most deceitful to us all."

"In what way, Lady Hart?" asked James politely.

"In not telling us that you were married to Pippi, of course. After all, we were your friends."

"There were very good reasons why I shouldn't tell my friends," said James coolly.

"Not all your friends, perhaps. But you might have told *us*."

"That's what all my friends will say."

She moved her shoulders impatiently, and began again: "Here you were, making love to Fran——"

But he interrupted her, pointing out mildly: "If you'll forgive my contradicting you, Lady Hart, I was *not* making love to Fran. In fact I was nearly killing myself not making love to her, because I knew I wasn't in a position to do so. I meant to see Pippi directly my leave was over, and arrange with her about the divorce we had promised each other, if ever either side wanted it; but in the meantime I suddenly realised that Pendock would ask Fran to marry him, long before I was free, and I thought it was at least fair to myself and to Fran, and even to him, perhaps, to tell her that I loved her too. Before I did so, I told her all about Pippi. She said she'd told you . . ."

She caught his arm with a swift gesture, looking round her anxiously: "For God's sake don't talk so loud, James; someone might hear you. . . ."

"What does it matter if they do?" said James, who had been speaking in his own soft, lazy drawl.

"Don't you see, James, that if the police knew that you had told Francesca about your marriage, they'd connect her with Pippi's murder. They'd think Fran killed her because she was your wife."

"It seems a very unlikely course for Fran to have taken," said James nonchalantly, walking along beside her, tossing a penny up and down. "I mean, I know she's an impatient person, but wouldn't she just have waited for a divorce?"

"She knew I would never let her marry you if you were divorced," said Lady Hart swiftly.

The penny missed a beat. He suggested diffidently: "After all—Fran's twenty-four."

"She would never have gone directly against my wishes." She added, as though to herself: "Besides, there was more to it than that. They'll think that when Grace Morland looked out of her window that night, and said she had someone in 'the hollow of her hand'— it was Fran she meant. Miss Morland hated Fran. I saw it that day in the drawing-room . . . not for herself, of course, but because she represented so many things that Miss Morland had never had and never known— and one of those things was Pen's love. The police will say that she saw you with Pippi in the orchard, James, and perhaps heard what you said; and that she saw how she could injure you and Fran, and that Fran silenced her."

He looked at her curiously. "Why Fran? Why not me?" and as she did not reply, he stopped walking and put away his penny and said earnestly: "Lady Hart—do you believe that I truly love Fran?"

She stopped also, and faced him squarely. "Yes, James, I do believe that."

"Then why don't you tell me what's in your mind?" he said. "What do you know about Fran that's frightening you? Couldn't you tell me? I might be able to help."

She eyed him dubiously and seemed to be taking a big resolution. She said at last slowly: "Very well. James, while Miss Morland was being killed down by the drive—Fran was not in her room!"

He swung round upon her. "Good God! Have you known that all this time?"

"Yes, all this time. I looked into her room before I went to call Pen, and she wasn't there. And afterwards she told us lies and said that she'd been asleep all the time. I've wanted to ask her, and I haven't dared. . . . James! It's haunted me night and day . . . where can she have been?"

He opened his mouth to speak and shut it again. After a pause he said: "If I tell you the answer to that question, will you answer a question of my own?"

She caught at his arm. "Anything, James, *anything*."

"Then why," said James, with great deliberation, "did you deny to Cockrill that you knew about my marriage to Pippi? You did know, didn't you? Fran herself had told you the day before."

She shrugged it aside indifferently. "I've already explained that to you. It was imperative that Fran shouldn't let Cockie know that she'd been aware of your marriage. He was separating us up and was going to interview us each, before we could say anything to one another; I took a leaf out of Pippi's book and tried to tell Fran, right under his nose, that I would keep silent about the whole affair. . . ."

James began to laugh. "You honestly don't know what a worry it's been to me. . . ."

"But Fran!" she said urgently. "Where can she have been that night, James? What can she have been doing? If you can tell me anything to set my mind at rest . . ."

"I don't know if it'll exactly set your mind at *rest*," said James, grinning, and he took out the penny and started to toss it again. "In fact it may worry you a good deal more than ever. You see she was sitting in the library canoodling with me!"

CHAPTER 6

The inquests upon the two victims were arranged to follow immediately after one another. Pendock and his guests were summoned to attend at ten o'clock the following morning, and there followed an anxious discussion as to whether or not Aziz would be permitted to enter. "Because if not, then either Venetia or I will have to stay at home with him," said Fran. "He can't be left alone, possibly."

"The servants'll look after him," said Pendock.

"He wouldn't stay with them," said Venetia earnestly. "He'd simply howl the place down. He won't be left with anyone except Fran or me; or Henry or Granny—he doesn't mind them."

"Thank you," said Lady Hart. "It's very good of him, I'm sure."

"People don't understand about dachshunds," explained Fran to the world in general. "They just love a selected few and they won't put up with anyone else. Will they, Venetia?"

"Aziz won't," agreed Venetia; "and Esmiss Esmoor wouldn't. She howled worse than Aziz."

"She did not," said Lady Hart indignantly.

"Oh, Granny, you only say that because Esmiss Esmoor was yours. She was simply frightful. . . ."

"Well, I'm quite sure that Aziz won't be allowed into the inquest," said Pendock, interrupting what threatened to develop into a heated argument. "And I don't think you'd better try and take him. The people here would think it was disrespectful."

They protested against any such suggestion. "By the way, ought we all to wear black?" asked Lady Hart, weary of Aziz and all his complications. "Would it look silly? I don't know what one does on these occasions."

102

"Of course we oughtn't to wear it," said Fran immediately. "It would be nothing but hypocrisy; we didn't like Miss Morland particularly and we didn't like Pippi at all. . . ."

Lady Hart sighed. "I shall wear my blue," said Fran.

Venetia quelled the storm of protest that followed this declaration. She said in her firm little voice: "That's going too far, Fran. That's making a parade of not being hypocritical, and it's almost worse. Nobody wants you to wear black cotton stockings and a long crape veil, but you must put on something quiet. Wear your fur coat and have a black hat and gloves and things. . . ."

It felt like going to church on a Sunday morning to be walking down the drive, all dressed up: the men in dark overcoats, Lady Hart in black, carrying her handbag like a prayer book, the girls in simple things, with the more cheerful notes removed from their hats. Bunsen walked at a respectful distance behind, and as they went through the village they were met with stares of interest and some hostility. Their reactions were characteristic, for Lady Hart was infuriated by it, Pendock contemptuous of it, Henry was made supremely uncomfortable by it, and Fran and Venetia did not recognise it at all; only James was both aware of the ill-feeling and totally indifferent to it.

They were met at the door of the tiny schoolhouse by the Vicar, a muscular young man, his clerical wings still damp from the seminarial egg. He advanced upon them, rather like the host at a garden party. "Good morning, Mr. Pendock. A very—ah—melancholy occasion; that's the correct phrase, I believe?" He affected a deprecatory smile, a jolly young fellow trying to do his Christian best with the indulgence of kind Mr. Pendock. Fran entertained the rest of the party with an almost imperceptible pantomime of being sick.

Pendock was a simple man at heart. He saw only a bumptious young chap doing his rather facetious best, and he shook hands and said that it was all a dreadful business, and he hoped it would soon be cleared up.

"You can imagine that it's not very pleasant for me, Mr. Plover, or for my friends. . . ."

Mr. Plover was by now goggling at the two lovely sisters, and he heard very little of what Pendock said, and contented himself by replying automatically: "Oh, very pleasant! Delightful!" which considerably astonished them all. At this juncture a car arrived bearing Mr. Ablett, the solicitor from Torrington, whom Pendock had requested to watch the proceedings on behalf of himself and his friends.

Mr. Ablett was a waggish, indiscreet little man, with a coarse, jolly laugh; he dug Mr. Plover in the ribs and asked him what he had been up to. "All for Mother Church, eh?" said Mr. Ablett in a gale of laughter.

"Mother Church?" echoed Mr. Plover faintly.

"Done pretty well out of poor Miss M., haven't you?" continued Mr. Ablett. "And now that Miss le May's followed her, you'll get her share too. No use suggesting, I suppose, that you should spend it on pulling down the church tower?"

Neither on the rugger field nor in his ecclesiastical college had Mr. Plover learnt to deal with jolly, common little lawyers. Pendock came to his rescue by taking Mr. Ablett gently aside and informing him that Miss le May's husband happened to make one of the party; and further asking, with curiosity, whether he were referring to the will.

Miss Morland's property had been divided into three legacies: a small life interest to Pippi, with reversion of the capital to the Church; a tiny income for Trotty under similar conditions; and the not inconsiderable rest to Pigeonsford Village Church, where her dear father had for so many years devoted himself to the souls of the parishioners. (Miss Morland's dear father had devoted himself to both soul and body of one of his flock in particular, a certain Miss Flossie Port, but had naturally not confided in his daughter Grace.) Mr. Plover looked smug, and Lady Hart said that it was no business of hers, but she did think the Church could have waited until poor, faithful Trotty had been seen a little more comfortably into her grave. Cockie, his new felt

hat already crushed out of shape, appeared on the
steps of the hall with the Coroner, Dr. Mear.

Dr. Mear had a flat grey face and his eyes swam like
colourless fishes behind his rimless pince-nez. He
liked to fancy himself Young at Heart, and con-
sequently treated anyone under thirty years of age with
a condescending chumminess extremely hard to bear.
Inspector Corkrill mumbled introductions.

Dr. Mear moved immediately into the more youthful
division of the little group, smiling benignly upon Fran
and Venetia, and holding James familiarly by the arm.
James looked down at him with a mildly bewildered air,
as though expecting him at any moment to slide back
into a rock pool. A press photographer ran backwards
and forwards in a sort of ritual dance, bending forward
to click his camera, give a satisfied smile, and dart off
again. Cockie said reluctantly: "This is not going to be
very pleasant, you know. You must all answer the truth
and leave it at that."

"Of course they will," said Dr. Mear brightly; and
added with an air of great humour and originality:
"Nothing but the truth!"

This remark appeared to lead nowhere and it met
with no response. Mr. Ablett looked at Dr. Mear with
loathing. Mr. Plover assured Fran that he knew that
sinking feeling well; he had experienced it many a time
before throwing the discus, up at Cambridge. At
Pigeonsford, Aziz broke away from the restraining
hand of the kitchen-maid, and started off down the hill
to the village.

The schoolroom had been divided to accommodate,
in uncomfortably close proximity, the nine true men of
the jury, the police, witnesses and press, and as many
of the public as could fight and jostle themselves into
two narrow benches at the back of the hall. They all
stood up, and there was a good deal of craning and
nudging as Dr. Mear strutted in and arranged himself
with some quite unnecessary fussing upon the dais
usually occupied by a downtrodden schoolmistress,
called (to the great delight of the youth of the village)
Miss Chambers. He rapped on the desk for order, and

clearing his throat which was already perfectly clear, opened the proceedings.

Dr. Newsome had not yet arrived, from which fact it became manifest to the assembled company that Mrs. Porter's sixth was about to do so. Dr. Mear, however, who could not be expected to care about any addition to the Porter family, was pardonably annoyed. A whispered argument ensued, followed by a loud cry from the Coroner's officer, which nobody could understand. A small black torpedo launched itself into the hall and on to Francesca's lap.

Fran and Venetia could not conceal their joy. "*Aziz!* Isn't he *clever*? Fancy finding his way right down here! . . . my heavenly one! . . ."

Dr. Newsome arrived, breathless and apologetic, but with a satisfied grin on his face; he marched up to the stand, gabbled the oath, and looked expectantly at the Coroner. Aziz emitted a joyful bark, for he knew Dr. Newsome well.

Dr. Mear looked over his glasses. "Is there a dog in here?"

"I'm afraid he's followed us down," said Fran, beaming proudly.

It made Dr. Mear feel quite a boy again, to see her standing there, clasping the dachshund in her arms, smiling at him over the sleek black head. He said irresolutely: "I don't think we can have a dog in here."

"Oh, he'll be perfectly good," promised Fran comfortably. "He won't do anything, now that he's with us. It's only because we left him behind."

A subdued murmur from the back benches caught the Coroner's ear, and the loudest and most frequent word was "disrespect." He said, more firmly: "I'm afraid it must be taken outside."

"He won't go," said Fran.

"He must go. Constable, take the dog out and tie him up near the door."

Aziz departed, looking back anxiously over the policeman's shoulder. Dr. Newsome embarked upon the history of his first examination and second, more detailed, one.

Dr. Newsome was blessed with an inoffensive self-confidence, and he found general practice in and around a small country town distinctly slow. In the absence of his father, the Police Surgeon, he had spent some happy hours in the mortuary, knife in one hand, text-book in the other, a junior colleague dancing excited attendance; and he was not at all averse to this opportunity of displaying his skill and observation. He had formed the opinion, he said, running his fingers over his bright gold hair, that the victim had been attacked elsewhere than at the spot where the body had been found. There were small abrasions on the shins and knees and he had found gravel embedded in them; this would seem to suggest that the actual assault had taken place on the gravel drive, and not in the ditch—because, you see, there was no gravel in the ditch. He looked up at the Coroner with an air of "what a good boy am I!" Cockie wished he would get on with it; he was not very fond of naïve young men.

Dr. Newsome got on with it. The body had been decapitated several minutes after death had occurred; a rather blunt instrument had been used which might well have been the hatchet which he now saw and examined (for the fifth time). He had at first thought that death had been caused by this instrument; but later he found injuries to the tongue and fracture of the laryngeal structures and hyoid bone which, though they might have been caused by the action of the chopper, often had a different significance; he had found the lungs to be engorged with blood . . . he went off into a dissertation upon the post-mortem appearance which was completely lost upon the jury and, in fact, appreciated by nobody but himself; finally it emerged that the actual cause of death was . . .

"Yes?" said Dr. Mear, leaning forward eagerly, his white false teeth sunk into his underlip. . . .

"Strangulation," said Dr. Newsome, and beamed round gaily upon the court.

Bunsen walked uncertainly up to the witness-box and there took the oath with respectful solemnity. He had left his sister's house in Tenfold village at 11:20 on the night of Grace Morland's murder. He knew it was 11:20 because as he bicycled out of the village the 11:25 train had left the station and begun its puffing ascent of the gradient that slopes gently up to the downs between Tenfold and Pigeonsford. It had taken him half an hour or a little more to do the four miles home; down in the valleys the snow was melting, but it had still lain, thin and treacherous, over the downs, and he was not as young as he used to be. As he turned in at the gate and pedalled up the drive . . .

There was a loud, thin wail from outside the hall, and everyone looked up, startled. "He's begun," said Fran to Venetia.

Bunsen smiled briefly and went on with his evidence. Ten minutes later Dr. Mear asked helplessly whether that noise could not be stopped.

"He'll be quite all right if you let him in here with us," said Fran readily.

This was impossible. She went outside and explained to Aziz that silence was really imperative, and he subsided, lying full length on the ground at the extreme end of his tether, his cold black nose on his forepaws, deeply depressed. Fran went back to her place.

Lady Hart gave a spirited description of her awakening by Bunsen. "He said: 'I was trying to get Mr. Pendock. There's a woman lying in the garden, down by the drive, near the gate.' I said: 'Who is it?' and he said that he couldn't see because her hair was all over her face. But he said: 'She's wearing Miss Fran's hat!'" She was unable to refrain from throwing a little dramatic effect into her recital. Her granddaughters greeted her upon her return to her seat with the declaration that she honestly ought to have been on the stage. They became slightly hysterical. Lady Hart sighed. Aziz lifted up his voice and wept.

Fran got to her feet again with a despairing gesture. "I'm awfully sorry, but if you'll just let me bring him in here, he can sit on my lap and he won't make a sound."

The murmur from the back benches grew into cries of "Shame!" Dr. Mear said testily: "I can't allow anything so disrespectful."

"I don't see anything disrespectful in it," said Fran heatedly. "What harm can it do Miss Morland to have him here?"

Dr. Mear's eyes swam like agitated fishes behind his pince-nez. "My dear young lady—that's not the way to speak. You must think of the feeling of friends and relatives, having such an insult offered to their dear ones."

"But they *weren't* dear ones," said Fran earnestly. Venetia tugged at her skirt. "Oh, well, all right; I'll take him home then, but I call it absolutely ridiculous. I didn't want to come in the first place, but I was made to; now it turns out I'm not wanted at all and I'm told to go somewhere else, just for a lot of false sentimentality. . . ." She marched out of the schoolroom, muttering like a schoolgirl. The back benches settled down again, deeply disappointed at so abrupt a termination to a legitimate grievance.

The inquest droned on. The owner of the hatchet deposed to its having been left beneath a tree just the other side of the stream, from where the body was found, and was very much aggrieved at being dismissed after only a minute in the witness-box, for he had bought a new suit entirely for the occasion. Dr. Mear drummed with his stubby fingers upon Miss Chambers' desk. Trotty was assisted up to the stand.

Trotty appeared to be quite unimpressed by Dr. Mear and his paraphernalia of law. She steadied herself against the edge of the witness-box, and holding the book in her pudgy white hand, took the oath in a voice of matter-of-fact calm. Mr. Ablett, evidently feeling that he must do something to earn his fee, jumped to his feet and suggested that the witness be allowed to take a seat; Cockrill, Dr. Newsome, Pendock, half a dozen policeman, and most of the members of the jury, who had been just about to make the same request, subsided with hurt feelings. The Coroner's officer tenderly assisted Trotty to a chair.

Trotty had been the last person, apart of course from the murderer, to see Grace Morland alive; that had been at about eleven o'clock, an hour before she had been discovered, dead. "Would you say that at that time she seemed troubled about anything?" asked Dr. Mear, rolling it like a telephone operator.

"Well, she wasn't herself, and that's a fact," said Trotty in her downright way. "She went off in the afternoon with her paints and rubbishes, as gay as you please, to do her picture of the church tower—though what she could want with another one, the dear knows, for if we've got one in the house we've got a dozen, but it's my belief and always was that it was nothing more nor less than an excuse to go up to the house. . . ." She ruminated in silence for a moment, and a little smile of kindliness and pity, and perhaps a shade of contempt, played about her lips, "But there—she's gone." She seemed to recollect herself, and added more firmly: "I didn't see her when she came back. A couple of hours later Miss Pippi arrived, and Miss Grace came out of her bedroom; I thought she'd been crying, but she was quite normal for the rest of the evening. At eleven o'clock, or a few minutes after— and don't ask me more nearly, sir, for I don't know within five minutes, and so I've told the police till I'm sick of the sound of it—I went to her room; she was sitting on the window-sill, with the curtains drawn back, looking out at the moonlight; and she turned round to me and she said, 'I've got her in the hollow of my hand, Trotty,' she said, but more as if she was talking to herself, and she curled up her hand, as though she held something in it, and she shook it a little, gently, and stared at it. . . ."

A hundred minds conjured up a hundred different settings: rooms with delicate pastel distemper, rooms with nice pink-flowered wall-paper, rooms with a dark-stained picture rail and innumerable water-colour sketches of the Old Church Tower; rooms with chintz-covered furniture, with mahogany, with oak; rooms with a deep soft carpet, with linoleum, with bare boards; but in each room the same little scene was enacted, the same little dumpy cripple stood with her hand on the light switch, the same tall, angular woman moved slowly forward, curling white fingers over something precious and hateful, held in the hollow of her hand; curling white fingers and staring down at them. Trotty got up abruptly and stumbled back to her place.

The press fought like demons for the privilege of being first to telephone to their editors that Miss Morland had met her death by strangulation, at the hands of a person, or persons, unknown.

The nine jurors chosen to attend the inquest upon the body of Miss Pippi le May, had, incited thereto by their wives and families, insisted upon their right to view the body of the victim; and their pea-green faces presented a remarkable spectacle as, after the luncheon interval, they sat wedged tightly together in the makeshift jury-box. Dr. Newsome, stroking his golden head, hopped merrily up to the witness-stand again. He had formed the opinion that decapitation had taken place at least some minutes after death had occurred; he could not say what weapon had been employed to sever the head. All other marks on the neck had been obliterated, but he had found fracture of the laryngeal structures and injuries to the tongue, which suggested throttling; also the lungs and right heart were engorged with blood. . . . At this point one of the jurors rose hastily to his feet, and there was a noisy interlude before he returned from the adjoining room, looking greener than ever and mopping his forehead with his handkerchief. Dr. Newsome went on gaily with the post-mortem findings. A second juror heaved into his handkerchief. "Perhaps we had better turn our attention to establishing the time of death," suggested Dr. Mear, who foresaw that further medical details were likely to prolong the session indefinitely.

Dr. Newsome had gone very, very carefully into the time of death. The victim had last been seen alive at just before eleven o'clock; he had examined her body at nine o'clock the next morning. He had found, he said, that rigor mortis was present as far down as the waist; the lower limbs were stiff, but this he thought might have been due to the extreme cold. Rigor mortis commenced, as a rule, in the neck and face, but of course in this case . . . The first juror showed signs of collapse, and Dr. Newsome passed hurriedly over the condition of the neck and face. In ordinary circumstances he thought the spread of rigor through the torso would have established death at about seven or eight hours previous to his examination; on the other hand the muscular state of the body made a difference and the health and strength of deceased would probably have retarded invasion to some extent. Also the low temperature in which the body had remained for at least some hours after death, must have assisted in retarding the stiffening; and all in all, he would say that death had occurred not more than eleven hours and not less than eight hours before his examination. As Pippi was known to have been alive eleven hours previously, and as the snow had stopped falling ten hours previously, this handsome exposition was less helpful than it might have been; and he further confessed that exceptions were so common and variations so incalculable that he could not be at all certain even of that. He nodded to the Coroner and stepped down off the stand. The jurors perked up considerably as they watched him depart.

It was extraordinary to see James going sheepishly through the rôle of Pippi's widower, to find him suddenly thrust into prominence in her concerns; the party from Pigeonsford House watched him with desperate sympathy. Dr. Mear made a little speech of condolence.

"Well, I'm afraid I can't quite accept that," said James, standing in the improvised witness-box, curling the brim of his hat with shaking hands. "I mean for years Pippi hasn't meant anything to me. We met occasionally in London, and I went to her shows and so forth, but I didn't love her and she certainly didn't love me. It's very kind of you to say all this, but I don't want to give you a false impression. . . ."

Lady Hart sighed again. These children. Why couldn't they keep their mouths shut, why couldn't they just accept the conventions at their face value and leave it at that? You could have too much of honesty and sincerity; there were penalties for being open and downright far in excess of the trifling discomfort of accepting sympathy, or admiration or respect or whatever it was, that you didn't happen to deserve. Why argue . . . why not just let it go?

Dr. Mear was scandalised. Husbands who lost their wives were prostrate with grief; people who died became, automatically, dear ones. Dogs were not brought into Coroners' Courts. He began to wonder whether there might not be something between this fellow Nicholl and the young woman who had spoken with a similar lack of feeling during the morning. His smile became less godly, and he shed his manner of kindly patronisation, and reverted sharply to business.

"Now—Mrs. Nicholl was a cousin of the deceased Miss Morland, wasn't she?"

For a moment James could not think who Mrs. Nicholl might be. He stood looking vacantly at the Coroner. "Mrs. . . . ? Oh, ah, yes. No, she wasn't."

"She wasn't what?"

"She wasn't a cousin of Miss Morland. You do mean Pippi, don't you?"

"Do you mean to tell me that Mrs. Nicholl, or Miss le May, which was her stage name, I believe, was not related to Miss Grace Morland?"

"No, I don't think she was. I remember when we were married something came up about it; she was originally in an orphanage till Miss Morland's mother sort of adopted her. . . ."

"Who were her parents, then?"

"I don't know at all," said James vaguely. "I don't think she did, either. I'm afraid she wasn't a legit, if that's what you mean."

Fran felt desperately sorry for him; he looked so casual and indifferent, standing there with his drooping shoulders, fumbling with his hat; but she knew that it was torture to him, that he could not bear to be standing before all these inquisitive people, dragging poor dead Pippi's name through what would, inevitably, become mud. She knew that he was blaming himself, searching his heart to discover whether he might not have been kinder to Pippi, better to her; asking himself whether he should have taken more responsibility in her affairs, looked after her more, somehow protected her from the terrible fate that had come upon her. Ridiculous, of course, Fran knew, for James himself needed more looking after than ever Pippi had done, tough little London sparrow that she had been; but there it was! Death did alter things, however matter-of-fact you might try to be. She lifted her head and smiled at him across the court, a big, wide, generous smile that had something in it of mockery because it had so much in it of tenderness. The Coroner intercepted the smile, and his questioning became more acid than before.

". . . perhaps you could tell us what was the subject of discussion at this meeting in the orchard?"

"The subject—oh, we were talking over getting a divorce."

"Indeed? A divorce. Would you tell us whether it was Mrs. Nicholl or yourself that wanted a divorce?"

James hesitated, and the hesitation was apparent to everybody in the court. "It wasn't so much a question of wanting it," he said at last painfully, "as of not getting it."

Dr. Mear was elaborately patient. "Perhaps you could explain that?"

"I mean that for a long time it had been understood between us that when either of us wanted it, we would get a divorce. I—I came into a little bit of money through the death of my uncle, a few days ago, and Pippi—my wife—came down to see me and tell me she was not so keen on the divorce idea after all." He spoke haltingly, and the perspiration stood out in little beads on his forehead.

"Was this on account of the little bit of money you had inherited?" asked Dr. Mear with heavy sarcasm, for everybody knew that the little bit of money amounted to several hundred thousand pounds.

"Well, I suppose it was. I had been making Pippi an allowance out of my own allowance, and it didn't amount to very much. I suppose she thought that it would be more worth while settling down and being properly married, now that I could have a home and so on. . . ." He raised unhappy brown eyes to the Coroner, and meeting a gaze of goggling excitement, looked hurriedly down again at the ruins of his hat.

"But you persisted in the desire for a divorce?" suggested Dr. Mear insinuatingly. James fell innocently into the trap.

"Yes, I did. I told Pippi I would make her as good an allowance as I possibly could, and certainly more than she would have got in alimony if she had divorced me."

"You were trying to induce your wife to give you grounds for divorcing her?"

"Well, not quite . . ." said James miserably.

"And what did she say to that?" asked Dr. Mear eagerly, ignoring this denial. He leant forward over the little desk, licking his smooth pink lips.

A sentence that Pippi had spoken clamoured in James's mind for utterance; clamoured because it had been locked up there in all its hard-bitten vulgarity, ever since his interview with her. He stammered wretchedly: "She said that she wasn't going to hand me over to—anyone—all tied up in a parcel, with blue ribbons. . . ."

Bunsen hobbled up to the box once more, when at last they let James go. He had left his sister a little earlier on the night of Miss le May's death than on the previous night. It must have been soon after eleven; but it was snowing hard and the roads were very bad; he had found it difficult to make his way along. He had been still on the crest of the downs between Tenfold and Pigeonsford village when the train had passed him, the 11:25 from Tenfold; he had seen its dark shape crawling up the rise that skirts the edge of Pigeonsford grounds. He had had to wheel his bicycle down the steep bit into the village. . . .

From midnight onwards Cockrill's men had guarded the house; two had paced the terraces all night, one had stood guard under Miss Hart's window, one had sat on the landing outside her room. This landing commanded a view of the doors to all the other bedrooms; the constable in question was positively certain that nobody had left his or her bedroom during the rest of the night; that nobody could have left by the windows, which were twenty feet from the ground; that he had not, even for a moment, dozed off or relaxed his vigilance. Cockrill wondered for a fleeting moment whether the gentleman did or did not protest too much, and came to the reluctant conclusion that he did not.

Mr. Ablett leaned forward alertly as Pendock went up to the box, but was unable to make any objections or offer any advice. How sweet Pen looked, thought Fran, watching him standing there, so straight and tall and handsome, with his little bits of grey hair just where actors put them, and his beautiful green-blue eyes; so—so dependable. Someone you could lean on, someone you could go to for comfort and security and shelter . . . not like James, who took so much of your tenderness and pity and gave you instead only a passionate longing adoration that bewildered you . . . who left all the caring and sheltering for you, on your side, to do. Pen was not twisting a hat to bits on the witness-stand; he looked very grave and sad, but he didn't wring your heart with desire to run to him and stand in front of him with outflung arms, protecting him against the cruelty and suspicion and nastiness of minds inferior to his own. There was pain in loving James, if you let yourself care for him; but Venetia had said that it was better just to be loved than to love too much . . . and here was Pen whom one had known from one's childhood, kind and dependable and safe and *strong*. . . .

Pendock gave unemotional evidence of his walk back to the cottage with Pippi. "She seemed perfectly normal, as far as I remember. Perhaps she was a little subdued: I think she was more upset than any of us realised by the death of her cousin—of Miss Morland. I said good-night to her at her door, and walked back to the house with the girl whom I'd sent down to sit with Miss Morland's maid."

Gladys was excited beyond measure at giving evidence. Mum and Dad and the kids was in the audience and Bert had promised to try and get the afternoon off. Not that she cared for Bert when Mr. Pendock was giving her his kind, brief smile as he passed her, going back to his place, saying in a low voice: "Don't be nervous, Gladys. Just speak the truth." Gladys assumed a Brave Smile and trotted up to the stand, her brassy locks furrowed into deep troughs by her recent perm. She made a good deal of capital out of her own kindly thought in tucking Trotty up in bed with a nice glass of hot milk. "Then the master arrived with Miss le May."

"Do you remember how Miss le May appeared? Did she, for example, appear quite ordinary to you?"

"Oh, quite ordinary, sir," said Gladys, wriggling a little, for her suspender belt was much too tight. "She didn't say anything particular, except that she'd left her glasses at the 'Ouse, and I told her that Trotty had found them and put them upstairs in her room, because, you see, she used to read in bed, Miss le May did. . . ."

"Yes, yes," said Dr. Mear impatiently. "I think we need not worry about the glasses. Then Miss le May offered you the use of her scarf?"

"Ever so sweet of her I thought that was," said Gladys, allowing a wistful smile to play over her lips.

Trotty gave deliberate evidence that she had already gone to bed when Miss Pippi came in from dinner at Pigeonsford House. She had had a sad and terrible day, following the discovery of the death of her poor Miss Grace, and she had known that Miss Pippi would not want her to wait up. She was very good-hearted, Miss Pippi was; sometimes she didn't think, but she was kind and considerate, really she was, poor girl. "People didn't quite understand her, sir, that's how it was. She said things quick and sharp, but she was good at heart . . ."

"So you heard her come in . . . ?"

Trotty knew that she had been interrupted because she had been rambling too much. The gentle, pitiful look was wiped from her face. She answered flatly: "Yes, sir."

"You didn't see her?"

"No, sir."

Dr. Mear was annoyed. "What *did* you do?"

"I went off to sleep, sir," said Trotty with a small triumphant smile.

Again she had been awakened, poor old Trotty, in "the middle of the night."

Once more the gentlemen of the press behaved like anything but gentlemen in their mad dash to the telephone. Verdict on Pippi le May: Strangulation by person or persons unknown. West End Actress Throttled. Well Known Revue Artist Decapitated. War or no war, Pippi was on the front page at last.

CHAPTER 7

Next morning the letters began to come pouring in.
Lady Hart had forty, mostly from old friends,
full of sympathy and horror and a good deal of pleasurable curiosity; Pendock had thirty; James had one,
from his Commanding Officer; Henry and Venetia, between them, had eleven; Fran had six: five of them
were from anxious and adoring young men, the last
was signed Mrs. P. Fitzgerald.

There were no more walks on the downs for Pendock
now. Cockie was brusque and ill at ease with him; he
did not disguise from himself that, had it not been for
the mysterious 'phone call that had at least started
while he stood talking to the others in the drawing-
room, the case against him would have looked very
grave indeed. He was in a state of acute nervousness,
missing his exercise and worried to death about Fran.
On the afternoon of the inquest he sought out Lady
Hart; she was sitting quietly in a chair by the drawing-
room fire, knitting a khaki sock. "On principle," she
explained, waving it at him as he came in through the
door. "I can't knit for toffee, but I feel I ought to
try."

"I wanted to talk to you about something," he said,
standing with his back to the high white Adam mantelpiece, looking down at her. "Do you mind?"

"Of course not," she said, glancing at him curiously
over the tops of her spectacles.

"It's about Francesca." He hesitated, absurdly reluctant to put into words the tumult of his feeling for
Fran. "I've fallen in love with her," he said lamely, at
last.

He looked so desperately anxious that she was almost at a loss for words. "I rather thought you had,
119

Pen," she said kindly. "It seems strange, after all these years. You've known her since she was a child."

"This has been going on for a long time," he said painfully. "Almost since she was in pigtails. I'm too old for her, of course, and I thought I could just put up with it and she needn't know anything about it; but now I find that it's got too much for me, and I can't. Would you mind if I told her about it and——" He broke off, and then said violently: "You can't think what it's like to know that she's in danger, to be so frantically worried about her, and not to have the right to look after her and protect her. . . . I'm going nearly mad with it. She's in my thoughts day and night, every moment of my life. . . . I must tell her and put an end to the uncertainty of it. Of course she won't marry me, but I think it'll be better to have the truth one way or the other, even if it's the other. . . ." He was silent, leaning back against the mantelpiece, his head bent, staring down at the floor.

Lady Hart was moved almost to tears, but she knitted steadily on and said after a moment: "You can but try, Pen. Fran has always been so fond of you. . . . I suppose it's possible that she might say yes."

He lifted his head, and for a moment there was such a light in his eyes that she added hastily, terrified of raising false hopes in him: "You know, of course, that James——?"

"Oh yes," he said. "I know that. But there have been dozens of Jameses and none of them have survived. He's a dear fellow, but he's too intellectual, too lackadaisical, too other-worldly for Fran. He won't last long."

"I'm not so sure," she said.

He looked at her again and then back to the carpet. "Well—I can take it that you won't object if I speak to her?"

"It was nice of you to have told me first," she said, smiling at him. "But you always were a person of the completest integrity, Pen. You know that with all my heart I wish for your happiness."

"I'll go now," he said.

Cockrill was standing in the hall, speaking to one of his men. Pendock was so much concerned with his own tremendous errand that he did not observe that both were white and shaken; he approached with a rather forced cheerfulness and said to Cockrill: "Do you think you could call your minions off for a little while? I want to talk to Fran. . . ."

Cockie swung round and glared at him. "Well, Fran has disappeared."

"Disappeared! What do you mean?" said Pendock.

"Disappeared—disappeared . . . can't you understand English, man?"

Something screeched and clattered in Pendock's mind. That red mist that had blinded him in his shrinking approach to the body of Grace Morland, descended upon him again; when he knew sanity, he was grasping the lapels of Cockrill's coat, and mumbling, over and over and over and over again: "Where is she? Where's Fran? What's happened to her?"

"This fool has let her go," said Cockie, shaking off his clutching hands.

Blue-green eyes blazed into frightened brown; but he said more coolly, turning upon the man: "Tell me what happened."

"She went in here, sir. I could hardly follow her." He indicated the cloakroom leading off the hall. "She said she wouldn't be a minute. When she didn't come out, I knocked and called. I broke open the door, sir. She isn't there."

A window was open, the net curtain fluttering inward. There was a mark on the painted sill, but outside the snow had melted right away, and on the stone terrace there were no prints of feet. "Anybody could have got in here," said Pendock, sick with dread.

"She may have got out," said the man.

"Got out! Why should she have got out? Where would she go?"

"She might have been sick of surveillance, Inspector," suggested Pendock, clutching at a straw. "She's so impulsive and independent and—and high-spirited. . . . Oh, my God! Fran!"

She was nowhere in the house. On an impulse Cockrill stumbled down to the summer-house at the bottom of the garden, and ran along the ditch by the side of the drive. When he got back, James was standing in Fran's room with an open letter in his hand.

"What are you doing here?" said Cockrill angrily.

"Reading a letter."

"What letter? Whose letter?"

"A letter from a Mrs. Fitzgerald," said James, folding it up and putting it into its envelope. "She lives at Monks Row, in Pigeonsford Village."

"For God's sake, man, who is this Mrs. Fitzgerald?"

"I've no idea," said James, opening his eyes very wide. "But she writes a filthy letter."

"Well, whatever it is, has it got a bearing on Fran's disappearance? I haven't any time to waste."

"It may have," said James, apparently quite unable to hurry. "She says she was at the inquest yesterday, and she makes some very low suggestions about Fran's behaviour there. She also suggests that Fran is what she calls my paramore, and she says that it's disgusting to see an English girl keeping a German dog. I think she believes Fran and Aziz are a couple of Fifth Columnists."

Cockie groaned aloud. "Well, what has this to do with her disappearance? Do you suppose that this woman has carried Fran off?" He looked round the room, frantically longing for action, yet unable to see any action he could take. "What has the letter to do with it?"

James looked surprised. "I thought you'd have seen my point; you know Fran almost as well as I do. . . . It wouldn't be like her to leave this letter unanswered, would it?"

Cockie sat down on the bed and mopped his brow. "You mean . . . ? You think . . . ?"

"Well, she isn't much of a hand at writing letters," said James.

They met her trotting up the drive, quite complacent and happy. "I do hope your bull-dog didn't get restive,

Cockie. I simply had to get away from him for a few minutes. I—I had some business to do in the village; as you wouldn't let me go there with anyone, I had to go by myself. I asked him to let me go to the huh-ha, and then I just hopped out of the window."

Cockrill was beside himself with rage. "You have given me and everybody else in the house a very bad fright indeed. Your grandmother's nearly off her head, your sister's distracted, Mr. Pendock's like a madman, and only your precious Captain Nicholl is as cool as a cucumber, choosing his words and drawling them out at the rate of one a minute. I've a good mind to put you in gaol for this, by God I have, Francesca!"

Fran was horrified, terrified, penitent. Tears poured down her face as she embraced them all in turn. "Darlings, I'm so sorry; I never thought for a moment that you might think something had happened to me. Pen darling, I'm so sorry; don't look so white and shaky, you're making me feel perfectly awful. Gran darling, I'm *so* sorry; Cockie dear . . ."

"Don't you so-sorry me," said Cockrill, flinging a newly rolled cigarette into the fire in his agitation. "You've behaved abominably, and if you didn't think, you should have. I've a good mind, a very good mind, to put you in prison; at least you'd be safe there, and out of mischief too. What were you doing in the village?"

Fran's face went pink. "I went to see a woman called Mrs. Fitzgerald. She wrote me a most horrible letter, and I had to go and tell her that she was wrong. . . ."

"Good God, child, because some evil-minded villager makes ugly suggestions about you and Nicholl . . ."

She looked at him through her tears. "Oh, it wasn't *that*. What does it matter if she thinks James and I have had an occasional bodge. It was much worse than that."

For one wild moment Pendock thought she was upset by the ridiculous things that had been said about her dog; but as he held out his hand to her, she flung herself into his arms and sobbed out against his shoul-

der that of *course* she hadn't meant to be cruel about
Pippi and poor Miss Morland, of course she hadn't
meant to sneer at them and suggest that nobody had
cared for them, or that they hadn't got any friends;
couldn't people understand that she only wanted to be
honest—not to be hypocritical, not to say a lot of
sloppy, idiotic things about them just because they
were dead. . . .

He knew that any shoulder would have done, that
she would have dragged anybody's handkerchief out of
their breast-pocket, and dried her eyes on it and smiled
up, sniffing gratefully, into their eyes. But he held her
in his arms, and she lay trembling against his heart;
and he was, for a little while, happier and more satisfied than he had been for many months past.

A man strolled unconcernedly into the little station
at Tenfold and asked for a ticket to Piddleport, the next
station along the line. It was a clear and moonlit night;
he spent the few minutes before the 11:25 was due, in
chatting to the porter-cum-ticket-collector, and when
the train came in, spoke a few words to the guard, and
climbed aboard. As they began to move he stood up on
the seat in the otherwise empty carriage and, removing
the blue-painted bulb from its socket in the ceiling, laid
it carefully in a corner; five minutes later he opened
the door of the carriage and climbed out on to the run-
ning-board; two minutes later he let go his hold and,
pushing himself backwards and away from the train,
tumbled into a ditch by the side of the line; one minute
later he was running, a hand clasped to his shoulder,
across the lawns towards the little summer-house in the
Pigeonsford grounds.

James knocked softly on the library door. "I say, Inspector, could I have a word with you?"

"Come in, Captain Nicholl," said Cockie cheerfully.
He was refreshed by a good night's sleep and, moreover, he thought that now, with a little more checking
up, he could lay his murderer neatly by the heels.
"What can I do for you?"

"I wanted to go into Tenfold," said James, with anxious modesty. "I wondered if you could just let me off for an hour or two. I'll take my watch-dog, if I must . . . in fact I'm getting so fond of him that I don't like to think of being without him."

"What do you want in Tenfold?" asked Cockrill, swivelling to and fro as gaily as a schoolboy in Pendock's desk-chair.

"Well, I wanted—to tell you the truth, Inspector, you'll think it very comic, no doubt, but I've got a rather snappy theory about how these murders were committed. I just wanted to work out the details, and then I'll tell you all about it—if you're interested."

Cockie grinned at him mockingly. "Well, well, well; you're turning into a Sherlock Holmes, are you? It may interest you to know that I also have a very interesting theory as to how the murders were done, Captain Nicholl; but as it doesn't concern you, I don't see why you shouldn't have a little jaunt. Your theory takes you to Tenfold, does it?"

James lowered his eyes and was understood to say that it was, vaguely, connected with Tenfold.

"All right. Go along. You needn't take Johnson, unless you're really so much attached to him that you can't bear to be parted. I make only one stipulation: that you don't mention this theory of yours to anyone else until I tell you that you may. Anything else you want?"

"No, no, rather not," said James, making joyfully for the door. "It's very good of you to let me go. Thanks awfully. Nothing else I want at all." He seemed quite animated.

"I thought you might want to borrow a bicycle," said Cockie, still with his mocking smile.

James had, as a matter of fact, already borrowed a bicycle. He pedalled majestically down the drive and through the village, and began the ascent of the downs beyond. Half a mile onwards, on the fringe of the rolling grassland, he came upon a solitary small disused hut and, dismounting, wheeled his bicycle in and propped it against the crumbling wall. A bus was com-

ing down the hill past Pigeonsford, and in ten minutes
would be through the village and climbing the hill towards him. He began to examine the shed.

Part of the roof was intact and would have kept the
earthy floor free from rain or snow. In the dry dust he
could distinctly see the marks of the treads of a bicycle
tyre; against the wall where his own borrowed machine
now stood, there were smears where another had re-
cently been propped; in the dust was a skid-mark as
though it had been lifted away from the wall, the wheel
brushing along the ground. He lit a cigarette and
strolled out on to the downs.

The bus overtook him and he signalled to it to stop.
Twenty minutes later he alighted in Tenfold village, and
making his way to the railway station, asked the time
of the next train to Piddleport.

The porter looked at him oddly, but vouchsafed that
there was one in an hour. "You don't get many people
travelling from here, I suppose?" said James with elaborate carelessness, and proffered a cigarette.

The porter refused the cigarette and replied that they
did not.

"What's the last train?" asked James, pursuing a
more definite line of inquiry. "Would that be the
11:25?"

The porter said that it would.

"Pretty empty, I suppose?" said James again, lighting his own cigarette. The porter replied that it was and
it wasn't.

James sighed patiently; this seemed to be getting
them nowhere, fast. He leant uncomfortably against
the doorpost, opposite what was fast becoming his adversary, and jingled the money in his pockets, searching for inspiration. Inspiration came.

"Those snowy nights there must have been nothing
doing at all?" he suggested, producing half a crown,
and beginning to toss it nonchalantly and catch it in the
same hand.

The effect was magical. There had been very little
doing indeed, said the porter immediately, thrusting
his cap to the back of his head and settling himself

more comfortably against his side of the doorpost. The
night that poor Miss Morland from Pigeonsford Cottage had been killed, had been very cold, though you
couldn't call it snowy: only 'arf a dozen people had
come on to the platform; most of them would be going
through to Medlicombe, he supposed, for that was the
only big station beyond Piddleport. No one he knew;
but then he hadn't been here long and hardly knew any
but the Tenfold people by sight. The next night was
colder still and really snowing 'ard. He remembered
particular, because only three people had caught the
train: a lady and a gent together and a gent who had
run on to the platform at the last minute and fair
snatched the ticket out of his hand and bolted into an
empty carriage. Pore old soul, he was puffing and panting that hard that the porter had made sure he would
bust a gut before ever he got aboard. He didn't remember having seen 'im before, unless it was on the
previous night—the night Miss Morland died—when a
rather similar old gent had made one of the six. He
wiped his hand across his mouth and opined that talking was always thirsty work.

So remarkable a collection and presentation of just
the facts he wanted, appeared to James to warrant as-
suagement of however handsome a thirst. He paid up
accordingly and made his way out of the village.

A great deal of questioning failed to elicit the ad-
dress of Bunsen's aged sister. He knew that she was
unmarried, but a Miss Bunsen was unknown to anyone
in Tenfold. He explained at last that the lady was old,
and very ill, and finally that her brother was butler to
Mr. Stephen Pendock of Pigeonsford House. The village rocked with laughter and informed him that he
wanted Miss Burner.

There was definitely only one lady answering to his
description, and James made his way, discomfited, to
Miss Burner's cottage. A district nurse opened the
door to him and said that that was nice, because now
he could sit with the patient while she popped out for
some Benger's Food.

Bunsen's sister reminded James a little of Lady
Hart, nor was she any less gracious or self-assured.
She received him charmingly, and there was a little
subdued merriment over his very natural difficulty in
locating her. Her brother, she said with affectionate
candour, was perhaps not very quick to take a joke and
had never quite understood; but years ago, when they
were little girls, dear Miss Venetia Hart, that was, and
her sister, Miss Fran, they had christened him Bunsen,
and she did believe that Mr. Pendock had forgotten that
he had ever had any other name. Hadn't the gentleman
heard his real name at the Inquest?

James's attention at the Inquest had been concentrated solely upon his own part in it, but he did not
trouble to explain this, for the old lady was rambling
on: "He's a good, kind brother to me, sir, indeed he is.
Ever so worried he's been over this illness of mine.
He's been over the last two nights, all through that
snow on his bicycle. . . ."

"I suppose you didn't *see* his bicycle?" asked James
eagerly.

Miss Burner looked astonished, as well she might.
"See it?—why, no indeed, sir. He left it in the shed, I
suppose, like he always does." Anyway, she'd been
pretty far gone, that first night; one of her legs was
very queer and she'd thought her time had come and
she was going from the feet up. A friend of hers had
lain four days, one day the right leg gone, next day both
of them, and then two days dying all the way up till it
came to the heart. The doctor had brought her, Miss
Burner, the very same pills as he'd given poor Martha,
small white round ones, and naturally it had alarmed
her very much; especially as with Martha it was the
stomach, while with herself it was the heart. . . .

James cut short this flow of reminiscence by saying
that he had come to ask Miss Bunsen—sorry, Miss
Burner—a question which was very important to him.
As he had disclosed at the inquest (Bunsen's sister
gave his arm a kind little sympathetic pat), Pippi le
May, his wife, was not in fact a relation of Miss Morland's at all. It had occurred to him that anyone who

had been as long in the district as Miss—er—Burner (got it that time!) would be sure to know something about her history. Everyone was talking about it and making wild guesses. . . .

Something changed in the old lady's face, and she said sharply that people had better let well alone or they might hear something they wouldn't like at all. "I would help you, Captain," she said, "but I mustn't say what I know and that's all there is about it. If it's any comfort to you, though, I will tell you this: Miss Pippi had for her father as good and kind a man as it would be possible to find. Her mother was not a good woman; she led him on, poor fellow, till he hardly knew right from wrong; he paid for it ever afterwards with sorrow and repentance and the fear of its being discovered— let alone with money. . . . But Miss Pippi, your wife, sir, she had his blood in her as well as her mother's; she was kind, she was, and generous in her way, and I always thought that that part she got from him. It may be a happiness to you to know, sir, now that she's dead, poor child, that her father, at least, was one of the best of men."

James crept out of the cottage feeling bitterly ashamed. If what he thought was true, then it would have been better for the poor old lady that her feet had, indeed, been dead on the night of Grace Morland's murder, that mortality had immediately claimed her legs and finally reached her heart after the fashion of death in Tenfold. But still greater issues were at stake than the peaceful end of one old woman, already at the gates of heaven; rather subdued he went back to the station and caught the midday train.

It was a very lovely day. All across the downs the birds were wheeling and singing, the snow was gone, and the little train puffed its way between rounded grassy hills, dotted with grazing sheep; they passed through Pigeonsford village and started up the gradient that forms the eastern boundary of the grounds of Pigeonsford House. James opened the door of the carriage and hung out over the line; as the train slackened speed, toiling up the long ascent, he relaxed his hold and jumped—tumbling, bruised and muddy, into the ditch. He picked himself up and made his way along the banks of the stream and out of the Pigeonsford gate.

He had twisted his ankle a little, but he limped off energetically through the village and up to the shed on the downs. People stared at his rumpled clothing, and he stopped and brushed himself down and straightened his collar and tie. No hurry, after all. An old man, a man with corns, would walk very slowly up the long incline.

His ankle hurt but he struggled manfully on. Once in the shed he would have the bike and there would be a long run down, and then only the little hill up from the village to the house. He wondered whether Bunsen had first killed his victims and then gone to fetch the bicycle, or whether he had brought it back from the shed before he got down to his dreadful work, and finally wheeled it up innocently to the house. In the case of Miss Morland, of course, he had left it by the body while he ran to fetch Pendock and lead him, full of false horror and lamentation, down to the dreadful scene.

The bicycle leant innocently against the wall of the shed. He hopped painfully on to it and sped down the hill for home.

Cockie was waiting on the terrace for him as he pedalled wearily up the drive; he said mockingly still: "Did you enjoy your ride?"

"No, I did not," said James, limping up the steps towards him.

"You seem to have had a tumble," said Cockie, full of hypocritical sympathy. He took him by the arm and helped him up the steps and into the house. "Have you hurt your foot?"

"Yes, I have," said James shortly, bewildered by his air of mischievous delight. "And if you knew what I've proved while doing so, you wouldn't be so much amused."

Cockrill led him into the ground-floor cloakroom and pushed him down unceremoniously on to the lavatory seat. "Let's have a look at it; oh dear, that's

nasty—quite swollen." He soaked a towel and
wrapped it tenderly round the injured ankle. "Just a
sprain, I expect." He added delightedly:

"There was a young man with a sprain,
Who fell off a bike—or a train . . .

but it was the train, wasn't it?"

James stared at him. "Did you see me?"

"No, I didn't see you," said Cockie airily, "but one
of my lads put his shoulder out doing the same thing
last night. It was a pity for you both that the line isn't
still banked up with snow—it would have been softer,
and not so far for you to fall. But still—you aren't an
old man."

James glared at him indignantly. "Do you mean to
say you'd worked it all out before I even started?"

"I can't say until I know just what you've discovered," said Cockrill blandly. "Did you find the porter
at Tenfold communicative? He's a bit of a money-grub-
ber, but I rang him up and told him to give you any
information you might require."

"Is *that* why he had it so pat?" said James dis-
gustedly.

Cockrill laughed. "I hope you didn't upset the old
lady?" he said, more gravely. "We were going over to
see her this afternoon, but I thought if I let you have
your head, you might get more out of her than we
should . . . being the bereaved husband, and all that."

James nursed his ankle, folding the cold towel
soothingly around it. "Well, honestly! Of all the ruddy
limits! You let me sweat all that way over, risking my
neck on that frightful old ramshackle, me that never
takes a yard more exercise than I can possibly help;
you let me chance Pendock's cook's bicycle being
pinched from that mouldy little shack on the downs,
you let me make a fool of myself all over Tenfold village
searching for a Miss Bunsen, and finally you calmly
allow me to endanger my life jumping off an express
train at ninety miles an hour. Damn it, man, I might
have fallen on the line and got myself cut in half, I

might have lain stunned in the ditch for hours and even drowned if there'd been any water in it; I might have broken my ruddy leg . . ."

But Cockrill was standing before him with a wild light in his eyes, grasping his soft white hair in both fists and muttering over and over to himself: "The weapon! . . . The weapon! . . . The weapon!"

James struggled up off the lavatory seat, and with the wet towel still wrapped round his ankle, hopped out into the hall. Cockrill was standing at the telephone asking urgently for Dr. Newsome. After a few minutes he said in a low voice; "That you, Doc?"

There was a slight crackling of the 'phone. Cockrill said impatiently: "All right; all right, I'm not going to keep you long. What a place this is for babies! Now, listen; in all your experience have you ever seen anyone that's been run over by a train?"

The telephone crackled again. "That's what I knew you'd say. But I think you *have*," said Cockie.

The telephone crackled for a long, long time. "I quite agree," said Cockrill at last, and put down the receiver with a bonk. He turned to James, still standing like a stork in one corner of the hall. "What are you doing here?"

"Thinking," said James, waking up with a start.

Cockie took his arm above the elbow and led him, hopping, into the library. "Oh, you were thinking. And what were you thinking, eh?"

"I was thinking that the 11:25 is the last train," said James, and sank down on to the sofa.

Cockrill produced the inevitable paper and tobacco and rolled a cigarette while he digested this proposition. "So it is," he said at last, turning to James with all the pleasurable excitement gone out of his bright brown eyes. "And a man can't jump off a train and shove a body under the wheels of the same train, can he? Not even if he has the body all ready to hand, he can't."

"Unless it was a very long train," said James.

"Well, the 11:25 is a very short train." He tittupped

on his heels, warming the seat of his trousers at the fire. "Besides, the body wasn't all ready to hand. I think you and I have been working too fast," he said.

"You mean you don't think that Bunsen—but look here, Inspector, he definitely left that bicycle in the shed. He biked up to the downs and parked it there; caught a bus over to Tenfold; stayed with his sister till twenty past eleven, and then caught the train back here; jumped off and into the garden at about twenty-five to twelve . . . in both cases it fits perfectly with the times of the murders; he'd save a good half-hour by taking the train; then he just fetched the bike . . . dash it, I saw the wheel-marks. I saw where the bike had leant up against the wall."

"You saw where *a* bike had leant against the wall," said Cockie, with a return of his impish grin. "Don't forget that my boys had made this trip before you."

James could not refrain from laughter at this simple explosion of all his fine conclusions. "You mean to say that the old boy rode solemnly into Tenfold, just as he said he did, and rode back again through the snow, and has nothing to do with it at all?"

"He must have. The girl was beheaded by the wheels of a train; they took her and held her there, after she was dead. . . ."

"But, dash it all, he *must* have been involved. He was Pippi's father—it's too much coincidence to suppose that he's out of the whole affair."

"Miss le May's father?" said Cockie, pricking up his ears and suddenly standing still. "Are you sure of that?"

"Of course I'm sure," said James eagerly. "His sister told me so. Miss Morland had found out, I suppose, and that's why he killed her. He was probably a little dotty after thirty years' solid remorse."

Cockrill turned and rang the bell by the mantelpiece. Bunsen came decorously in and stood by the door. "You rang, sir?"

"I want a word with you," said Cockrill, beckoning him into the room. "Shut the door behind you. Now, just tell me this: you've been in Pigeonsford and the district a very long time? Your sister has just given us information as to the parentage of Miss Pippi le May and I want your confirmation. What do you say?"

Bunsen looked astounded. He held his trembling old hands stiffly at his sides and kept his eyes on the floor. "Well, if she's told you, sir, I suppose she had good reason. She wouldn't have done it without, for she swore, thirty years ago, that nothing should ever come out about it in the village, and to this day I don't believe anything ever has. I hope, sir, you won't think it necessary to publish this? Mrs. Morland knew, of course—Miss Grace's mother, that was—but she was a saint, poor lady, and she made allowance for 'uman frailty. She got the child into a home, and later on, after the Vicar died, she had her in the house and gave out that she was a niece of his, or somethink of that. Miss Grace never knew the truth; she was a good woman, Miss Grace was, but not like her mother. Mrs. Morland was a saint, she was."

"And the mother?"

"The mother was a woman called Port, sir. She was a bad lot, though she was buxom and pretty; she left the village at the time, and she died long ago, I believe. Anyway, she never troubled the child nor the Vicar again; he sent her money, of course, and he provided for the child. . . ."

"The Vicar?" said James and Cockrill, staring at him.

"Why, yes, sir; poor gentleman, he was a good, sweet soul, but he'd been a high living lad, and the woman got hold of him . . . mind you, he was quite a young man at the time. My sister was midwife here, sir, that's how she knew of it all, for Flossie Port she went to ask her about her condition. She and I were the only people outside the family that ever knew what had happened. We promised the poor Vicar, and we promised Mrs. Morland again when she died, that never would we breathe a word; and only that my sister's seen fit to tell you now, sir, I shouldn't have said anything about it. I hope you won't let it come out . . . it would be a shock to the people in this village, sir. . . ."

Cockie, recovered from his astonishment, gave such comfort as he might. "I don't think that will be necessary, Bunsen; I'll keep it all a secret if I possibly can. Your sister didn't actually say in so many words what had happened, but from what she did say it was easy to conclude that it was—the Vicar. Wasn't it, Nicholl?"

James shot up off the sofa. "Yes; yes, rather. We won't breathe a word, Bunsen. Don't you think, Inspector," he added, looking imploringly at Cockrill, "that it would be better if Bunsen were to say nothing to his sister about this little talk? It's only just clearing things up. I don't see that it need be repeated at all."

Cockie, smiling grimly, was in complete agreement. James put his hand on the old man's sleeve. "There you are, now, Bunsen; don't you worry any more. The whole thing's over and done with. Don't let it upset you; it's finished."

Bunsen beamed at him gratefully. "Thank you, sir. Thank you, Inspector. You're very good, I'm sure. I wouldn't like to think that after all these years the poor Vicar's name should be dragged through the mud. . . ." He shuffled off, wagging his head with relief, all unconscious, blameless old man that he was, that for some hours he had been, in the eyes of at least two people, three times a murderer, and once of his very own child.

CHAPTER 8

A young man sat dejectedly upon the narrow bed in a cell at the police-station at Torrington, his head in his hands. For nearly six months now he had been driving himself to confess to the murder of Lily Baines, that night last summer, in the little copse; and now he was here and had confessed and nobody would believe him. He had met her in Torrington in a shelter, the time they had the false air-raid alarm; he had looked after her and seen her on to her bus when it was all over, and she had promised to meet him again. She had said she was a seckerterry to a rich lady in Pigeonsford village; he had read afterwards in the papers that she had only been a kitchen-maid—but, anyway, seckerterry or kitchen-maid, he had fallen in love with her, really in love, nothink wrong about it, and after several meetings in Torrington he had made an assignation with her one night in the little wood near where she worked. She had arrived there with a young man who had kissed her and gone away. She had explained that this was her brother; but afterwards, when he had asked her to marry him, she had confessed that it was not her brother at all, but her steady; that they had been walking out for two years; that all this had meant nothing to her but a couple of dates for the flicks and a meat tea at the Regal Palais. She said she had told nobody about their meetings, because she was afraid of her steady finding out. She had gone on and on talking. He did not know what she had said after that, for something had gone very funny inside him, like a sharp knife cutting slowly, with a sickly warmth, into his very flesh. . . . Then he had seen the scythe leaning up against a tree, near the churchyard wall; she must have read in his eyes that he was going to kill her, for she had begun to be frightened and to plead with him and beat him off with her hands; he had put his arm round her and held her still, taken off her belt with the other hand and tied her with it. After—it—was all over, he had found her brooch in his hand. It was a cross of diamonds and rubies; he had given it to her himself, and it had cost three-and-eleven. He had laid it very gently on her breast, reverent like. The gentlemen must believe that he had been sorry by then for what he had done. He had never meant her no harm. He had never been in love before.

"You're telling lies," said Cockrill.

"I'm not, sir," said the young man earnestly, for having taken this great and terrible decision, it was dreadful to be in suspense all over again as to whether or not he would be hanged for a murderer. "As true as I'm here I killed the girl, and I laid her down at the foot of the tree, and I put that there cross on her chest to show I was sorry, like. . . ."

"The brooch was lying crooked on her breast, with the pin upwards," said Cockrill sardonically. "That doesn't sound much like reverence, does it? You're telling lies, my son."

The family up at Pigeonsford were lingering over after-dinner coffee. Cockrill sat down gloomily at the end of the table and accepted a cup. "That fellow we're holding at the station—he's a fraud. Out for sensation or notoriety, I suppose."

"He *did*n't kill the girl in the copse?"

"No. He's telling lies."

Hope lit up their faces. "Then the original murderer may still be loose? There may still be an outside person to have killed Miss Morland and Pippi . . . ?"

"I never believed otherwise," said Lady Hart austerely.

"Oh, but Gran, it looked so pec*u*liar. I mean, this man might have killed Miss Morland, but of course he had given himself up by the time poor Pippi . . . It was too much to hope for two maniacs, one to be in gaol and one to be murdering Pippi; you must say it was *too* much coincidence. It had to be one of us."

"Fran—don't say such things!" said Pendock.

"Well, but it's all right to say them now. Of course, if this man's just a loony, wanting publicity, then the original murderer's still at large, and he killed Pippi and Miss Morland, and there's nothing more for us to worry about." She got up and poured out more coffee for Cockrill, leaning over his chair. "How are you so sure this man's telling lies, Cockie darling?"

"He's been adding a bit too much embroidery, like they always do," said Cockie crossly, for several potential suspects in the bush were a lot less satisfactory than one in the hand. "He'd read it up in the papers and he'd got it all pat; but he slipped up on one small detail about the brooch, which he need never have mentioned at all." He looked at Pendock over the rim of his coffee-cup. "You remember the brooch? A vulgar little red-and-white cross?"

"I wish I could forget it," said Pendock sadly. "I picked it up while I was waiting with Brown, for you and the police-surgeon. You know how it is, one has these unaccountable impulses—I stooped and picked it up off her body and held it in my hand. There was blood on it: for weeks I felt as though I could never wash it off."

"You picked it up?" said Cockrill, putting down his cup with a rattle in its saucer.

"Yes. It didn't matter, did it? I put it back again immediately."

"When you say you put it back—you just threw it down on to the girl's body?"

Pendock looked grieved. "Well, not exactly threw it; but I did just drop it back, rather hastily. I was so shocked to find the blood on my hands."

"And how was it lying when you saw it first?" asked Cockie, leaning forward intently.

"It was lying in the middle of the girl's breast, quite neatly: the right way up and the long end pointing toward her feet. Now that I come to think of it, it looked as though it had been placed there like that, because it *was* a cross. It never occurred to me before: should I have mentioned it at the time? Is it important?"

"It depends what you call important: it's going to hang a man," said Cockrill, and got up and left the room.

They gazed at each other in stricken silence. Pendock put his head in his hands. Fran said defiantly: "So it *was* one of us!"

"Oh, Fran darling, don't."

"Well, we were all quite ready to admit that that was the only alternative, when we thought the 'outside' person was at large; but now we're involved in it all over again."

Lady Hart leant her head on the palm of her hand. "Where's it all going to end? When will it all be over . . . ?"

"It had better be over pretty soon," said James comfortably. "I'm supposed to be in the Army, even if I *don't* know which hand to salute with, and they'll be getting restive if I'm away much longer. You people don't seem to realise it, but it's a dreadful thing for an officer and a gentleman to be running around the countryside like a hunted thing, with detectives at his heels."

"Not running, darling. Bicycling."

"No mockery from you, Venetia," said James severely. He held out a piece of walnut to Aziz. "I wouldn't touch it, old boy. It's German!"

Aziz immediately ate up the piece of walnut and looked for more. "There you are—he *does*n't do it!"

"He does it for us," said Fran indignantly. She proffered a hazel nut, saying in a sharp, high voice: "It's German!"

Aziz advanced resolutely upon the hazel nut. "It's British," cried Venetia, just in time. They fell into ecstasies at his cleverness.

James, having brought a smile back to the eyes of his beloved, relapsed into a torpor. Henry, however, was not so easily to be balked of a nice round discussion. He said thoughtfully: "If we could only prove that

Pippi could have been killed after the snow stopped falling."

"It wouldn't make any difference," said Fran immediately.

"It might. Suppose we could find a way that it could have been done, and then show that it *had* been done that way, then it would prove that none of us could have been involved, because of course the house was full of policemen from midnight onwards, after it stopped snowing."

"It *is* a point, darling."

Henry got to his feet. "What about all going down to the scene of the crime?"

"And letting poor Bunsen clear away," said Lady Hart. As they humped themselves into overcoats, scarves and furs, she added quietly to James: "Do you hate this? Would you rather we didn't go?"

James looked surprised. "No, I don't mind. Because Pippi was my wife, you mean?" He gave himself away a little by adding: "I think it's best to look the thing right in the face; no use pretending that it hasn't happened. One has to try and be sort of—impersonal."

"It relieves their nerves," she said, looking after the girls as they walked across the grass between Henry and Pendock. "This is rather a nightmare for ordinary people, James dear; and if they didn't make a sort of hectic game of it, I think we'd all go mad. That's the reason Henry's doing it; and that's why I rather encourage them. . . ."

"Don't mind me," said James, but without bitterness.

Henry was saying, looking about him eagerly: "All we have to do is show Cockrill that it could have been done."

Fran, her hand tucked into Pendock's arm, peered out from under her scarlet hood: "Well, go on, darling. You show!"

"What'll you bet I can't?"

Lady Hart advanced with James, and halted on the banks of the little stream, beyond the summer-house. "Henry dear, curb your propensity for money-making, and give us a straightforward explanation, if you've got one to give, which I don't for a moment believe. And just bear in mind that after all Pippi was James's wife.

Henry's warm Jewish heart overflowed with remorse. "I'm so sorry, James, old boy. I—it's all such a muck, Cockie telling us that the murderer *is* caught and then that he *is*n't, and one's nerves get jangled up and one forgets that after all this is a terribly personal matter. Let's call it off; I'll work it out some other time."

James wished that people would not keep reminding him that Pippi had been his wife, and that, somehow or other, he seemed to have let her down. It was hard for Fran too. He knew that, under her brittle raillery, she was hurt by every reference that he had been in love with someone else, had married someone else. He took her arm and said, in his careless drawl: "Let's pretend we're investigating the murder of someone none of us knew. I owe Pippi something because she was once, long ago, my wife; so we'll leave her out of it altogether, and Henry will convey an inanimate object—a bag of golf-clubs or an overcoat or something—to the summer-house, and come away again, leaving no traces on what ought to be the snow . . . as I suppose that's what he's going to prove he can do. . . ."

Constable Troot obligingly returned to the house for a great-coat, and, with sundry dark hints, borrowed from the cook a long, stout piece of rope. "Who can cope with a lasso?" asked Henry, busily tying knots.

Nobody was much good with a lasso. The constables unfroze, literally and figuratively, and entered into the spirit of the thing; one of them finally got the noose over the lightning-conductor of the summer-house, and another tied the opposite end of the rope to the branch of a large old tree growing on the banks of the stream.

"You've got to get to the railway line and back," said Fran, alarmed by the sight of these preparations for the safety of a privately staked half-crown.

Henry indicated the wide sweep of the lawns with an airy wave. "Nothing easier. No ropes, no mirrors, nothing up my sleeve. Like to take a bye on it?"

Fran looked round the garden, bewildered. "From here to the railway line? And no rope? I don't believe you can do it."

"Well, then, why don't you bet? Half a crown on the side?" He produced a huge pair of gum-boots from the folds of the overcoat and waded into the stream.

The stream led up to the railway line, dived under it and reappeared in the meadows beyond. Henry paused at the low viaduct, reaching up to lay the overcoat for a moment across the line; respectful of James's feelings, he pulled it hurriedly down again and threw it over his shoulder. Half-way back down the stream, he halted at the tree where the rope was tied and began to scramble up. "Need I keep these boots on? They're miles too big for me."

Venetia was terrified. "Darling—you're not going to try and tight-rope it?" She ran out under the sagging rope. "Henry—Henry darling, don't be silly. Don't do anything funny. You know you'll fall off!"

He looked down, laughing, from a big safe branch. The rope stretched between him and the summer-house. "All right, sweetheart, I won't make a martyr of myself for the sake of Fran's half-crown. Move out of the way . . . here we come!" He grasped the rope with both hands and swung out, hanging at arms' length, and started slowly to work himself along.

It was easy to drop into the open space at the side of the summer-house. He laid the overcoat on the seat, to look as little as possible like a propped-up body, and climbed out again on to the rope. "Are you going to make me get all the way home again?" he called, peering down at them from between his upstretched arms. "I've proved what I set out to prove. My arms are nearly out of my sockets; do let me off the rest!"

Venetia felt within herself a tiny, involuntary recoil. He looked like a little black monkey, swinging himself along hand over hand, grinning and chattering at them, imploring to be let down. She wished he would not make himself so cheap and ugly and ludicrous; his black eyes were shining with excitement in the cold, clear moonlight; she knew that he was enjoying himself, and yet that if she had run out under the tree and told him so, those heartless eyes would have melted at once into remorse and sympathy. Mysterious, intangible creature, whose depths she would never understand . . . elusive, gay, charming, adorable creature whom, for ever, she must passionately love. For the hundredth time she stifled the realisation that, of all the people about her, she could most readily imagine Henry a murderer.

They were helping him down, laughing and chattering, all but herself and Pendock. Pendock said gravely: "God knows what this is going to mean."

James was always, in his idle way, the steadying influence; with a tendency to prick Henry's bubbles for the pleasure of hearing them pop. He said: "It's interesting, but I don't see that it proves anything. You got there with an overcoat, but a body's a different matter. Pippi was small, but she was muscular and she had rather big bones; she'd have weighed quite a lot. It nearly killed you doing it with a weight of, say, ten or twelve pounds. You couldn't do it with more."

"*I* couldn't," said Henry, examining his blistered hands. "But then, I'm on a small scale, and I haven't got the English respect for the Bicep; I detest outdoor games and messing about with dumbbells and things. *I* couldn't have done it; but I still believe that it could have been done—by someone with very strong arms. It would have to be a pretty hefty man, or a—a gorilla, or a . . ."

"Or a trapeze artist," said Pendock, and turned away from them and walked off slowly up to the darkened house.

A trapeze artist! Cockrill, stumping back up the drive, paused in the shadows, electrified by Pendock's words, carrying clearly in the cold night air. Trotty! There it had been all this time, staring him in the face. Trotty, who had known both Grace Morland and Pippi from their childhood, who might have had a thousand reasons for wishing to murder them. He recognised, all of a sudden, a likeness between Trotty and Pippi, their rather large heads and carroty hair, a length of body that had made them appear a little out of proportion, a certain toughness, both physical and mental. . . . He wondered if Trotty could be in any way connected with the woman who had been Pippi's mother; she had always cared more for Pippi than for the fastidious, smug, self-righteous Grace.

Trotty! Grace Morland *had* told her, of course, about the hat. Perhaps she had sneered at Fran, had said filthy things about her, as she had to Pendock. Trotty was fond of Fran and Venetia. She would have seen Fran and James in the orchard, would have put two and two together and deduced that open back door; would have come up to the house and taken the hat from the hall-stand, while they stood and talked beneath the fruit trees; would have thrust it upon the head of her murdered mistress, crying with insane derision: "There, take that, you self-satisfied hypocrite . . ." and, laughing perhaps, or weeping, would have scrambled away on pitiful, twisted legs. . . .

And Pippi had seen it all, or part of it, so Pippi had had to die too. Trotty must have followed Pendock back to the house that night, after he had seen Pippi to the cottage, hurrying after him with the jerking, crabwise movement that filled one's heart with pity and disgust; she would have stood there quietly at the front door, holding it a little ajar, watching Pendock dismiss the maid, watching him put the scarf into the drawer, watching him go off to the drawing-room. She must have slipped in at once and gone to the telephone—on what mad impulse nobody could know—and put through her call to himself, standing there impatiently, one ear cocked for the opening of the drawing-room door. There hadn't been much time, but she could have put down the receiver quietly and snatched up the scarf and been out of the front door before Pendock had finished his good-nights; and all he had had to do was to lock the door after her.

He crossed the bridge that led to Pigeonsford Cottage.

Pendock was sitting in the drawing-room when they all got back to the house, staring into the fire; he looked very white and strained. As Henry plumped himself down on the sofa beside him, he said, with a sort of illogical resentment: "I suppose you're going to go running to Cockrill with this—discovery?"

Henry was astonished at the tone of his voice, but he said lightly: "The discovery's all washed up. We couldn't get the rope off again!"

"You couldn't get it off?"

"Not from the stream; and of course if we'd gone nearer, the marks would have shown in the snow. I suppose Trotty, with her circus training, might conceivably have got the lasso round the lightning conductor from the stream, but she couldn't have got it off—the noose just tightened round the base of the thing."

"It needn't have been a slip-noose," said Pendock doubtfully.

"We tried the other way, too. It can't be done."

Pendock was silent, his heart warm with joy for poor old Trotty, who was not a murderess after all; even if it did leave now, all over again, only the six of them: himself and Lady Hart and Fran and Venetia and Henry and James. James was saying vaguely that perhaps she hadn't got the rope down, but had just tossed it all up on to the roof of the summer-house.

"No, no; the police would have found it. They looked up there for the weapon."

"Anyway, the whole thing was rather potty," said Fran, sitting Aziz upright on her knee and lovingly stroking his tummy. "Just because Trotty's arms may still be strong, it doesn't mend her legs, and she's been like this for too many years for it all to have been a put-up job. I can remember, when we were little girls, seeing Trotty starting off before everybody else to get to church in time on a Sunday morning; and propping

herself up against the counter in Maggis's while she did
her shopping . . . can't you, Venetia?"

"Of course," said Venetia joyfully, for she too was
glad that Trotty was safe.

"Anyway, that'll be five bob from you, please,
Fran."

"It will not be anything of the sort," said Fran, putting down Aziz and preparing to give battle. "You said
you would prove that the murderer could have done it
that way, and you've failed. I'll pay up the half-crown
for the wading-in-the-stream idea, because I think that
was good; but I'm not going to fork out the second
one, definitely."

"I proved that the murderer could have got to the
summer-house and back. . . ."

"Yes, but he couldn't have got the rope down. . . ."

"I never said anything about getting the rope
down . . ."

James lay back in a big arm-chair, looking on from
beneath his lazy eyelids. "What do *you* think, Jimmy?"
said Fran, working her way towards him on her knees.

Lady Hart and Venetia and Henry were involved in
a heated argument. James bent forward and took her
hands in his. "I think you're the loveliest little thing on
God's earth," he said.

She knelt before him, laughing and blushing, and
looking up into his face. "James *dar*ling—someone'll
hear you!"

He did not laugh. "Fran, does it matter if they do?
Just say you'll marry me, Fran, and all the world can
know that I think you're the most exquisite, adorable,
desirable woman that ever drove a man mad with longing. Dear Fran, sweet Fran, my lovely heart, tell me
you'll marry me; one day when all this is over, even if it
is in this dreadful way that I've become free to ask you
. . . do say you'll marry me, Fran?"

She looked round her anxiously, pulling her hands
away from him; the three contestants wrangled over
her bet; Pendock lay back on the sofa, his face in the
shadow. She scrambled to her feet and, as she moved,
stooped forward and gave James a little fleeting kiss on

the corner of his mouth. "I might," she said; and a moment later was defending her second half-crown.

Pendock sat silent in the shadows, blind with pain and jealousy and a desperate sense of defeat. He did not look up as Cockrill came into the room and took up his favourite attitude before the fireplace, fishing for papers and tobacco. Cockrill said abruptly: "I've just been down to the cottage to see Trotty."

"It wasn't Trotty," they all said quickly.

"You don't say so?" said Cockrill, with an edge to his sarcasm all the more keen because he himself had been fooled by the easy coincidence of the rope and the trapeze artist. He added sweetly: "And you all realise what that means?"

"That it must be one of us?" suggested Fran.

Cockrill took a big resolution. He said, staring thoughtfully at the tip of his cigarette: "If I could prove to you that it was one of yourselves—what d'you suppose you would do?"

"What would we *do*, Cockie?"

"What would the rest of you do?" said Cockie impatiently. "You're all very good friends; most of you are more to each other than that. What would the others do if I told you that one amongst you was a murderer? Whose side would you be on? Would you stick by him—a man who had killed a woman and cut off her head?"

"A man?" said Lady Hart, staring at him.

"A man or a woman," said Cockrill irritably. "Can't you use your imaginations? I'm speaking in the wide sense. What would the rest of you do about it? Would you give him up to justice?"

"It wouldn't be anything to do with us," put in Henry calmly. "If you knew the truth, we couldn't protect him anyway."

"I might not be able to prove the truth," said Cockie, intent on his cigarette.

"Are you suggesting that we should help you to prove it?" asked Venetia indignantly. "Do you think we would turn against each other . . . ?"

"Not in the case of murder and mutilation?"

They were silent. "Perhaps it depends on the motive," said Lady Hart at last.

"The motive in this case was fear."

"But fear of what?" said Fran.

"Fear for your safety," said Cockrill. He lifted his head suddenly from the contemplation of his cigarette and said steadily: "Wasn't it, Mr. Pendock?"

Pendock sat motionless and did not speak. Two of the police guard moved a little nearer. Fran said, going straight to the heart of the matter: "But the person who telephoned—that wasn't Pen! He was with us in the drawing-room when the woman started telephoning to you. There *was* a seventh person involved! It couldn't have been Pen. And if she could have telephoned, why couldn't she have murdered Pippi, too?" She jumped up and stood before Cockrill at the mantelpiece. "Of *course* it wasn't Pen. Of *course* it was the woman who telephoned that killed Pippi le May."

"Have you ever considered," said Cockie, looking straight at her, grimly derisive, "that the woman who telephoned was Pippi le May herself?"

"*Pippi!* The woman who telephoned? But she said she was the murderer of Grace Morland."

"Perhaps she was," said Cockrill, and started on another cigarette.

They stared at him, stupefied. He said quietly: "I'll tell you a little story; shall I, Mr. Pendock?"

Pendock's silence was the worst thing of all. He made a tiny motion of his hand, cigarette between two fingers, as though to say: Carry on. *I* don't care.

"It's the story of a—we'll call him a fairy prince," suggested Cockie, looking round at them with his little, mocking, bright dark eyes. "He was a very good, upright prince, and he was, of course, in love with the customary fairy princess.

"One day there came to the prince's kingdom something unimaginably evil, a creature of some darkness that we don't quite understand, and she killed one of the prince's people and cut off her head and flung her into a ditch—perhaps one day we shall find out why.

And then she remembered something that her victim had mentioned earlier that day, and she crept up to the prince's palace and through the back door which a certain young couple had left open while they did a little spooning in the orchard at the bottom of the prince's garden; and she took from the palace the princess's little ridiculous hat, and armed with this hat she added a final, mocking insult by thrusting it on to the head of the poor mutilated corpse in the ditch."

"You are positively lyrical, Inspector," said James from the depths of an arm-chair.

Cockrill ignored him. "And the next evening, because there was no such unfairy-like thing as a telephone in her home, the murderess came up to the palace and, standing in the hall, rang up the police-station and said, gloating in her madness, that the fairy princess was 'next.' And while she still held the receiver in her hand, the prince came out into the hall."

He paused. Pendock spoke for the first time. "What did he do?"

Cockrill swung towards him and looked him in the eyes. "What would *you* have done?" he said.

Pendock did not answer. "This is what my prince did," said Cockie, rocking backwards and forwards gently, warming the seat of his trousers at the fire. "In his horror and rage, and in his deadly fear for his beautiful princess, he went up to the creature and put his hands round her throat and choked the life out of her. What he did next he did, perhaps in anger, or perhaps to disguise his actions and make them appear the work of the maniac who had gone before . . . he heard the whistle of the train and, dragging the body out through the falling snow, he lifted it on to the line and let the train run cleanly across the neck; and then he carried head and body to a place where they would not be found until the following day, and left them there. I don't know why he tied the head back to the body with a scarf. Perhaps it was revenge for the business of the hat; perhaps it was with some vague idea of putting off discovery a little longer by making it appear that a live woman sat in the little summer-house . . . but of course *he* would have known where to look for the scarf."

There was a long, long silence. Pendock drew upon the stub of his cigarette and flung it into the fire. He said at last: "How long is it since you got all this worked out?"

"Since I saw Trotty this evening; she happened to mention that, according to your maid Gladys, Pippi le May said on the night of her death, that she had left her glasses up at your house."

"What has that got to do with it?" said Pendock.

"She hadn't left them there."

"I know. Gladys told her that they were on the mantelpiece in her own drawing-room."

"She knew that already," said Cockie.

"Well then, why did she say she must come back to Pigeonsford and get them?" Light began to break and he answered his own question: "I see. You think she wanted a reason for getting back into the house?"

"She wanted an excuse if she were found in the house," said Cockrill. "She was going to use your telephone."

"Why didn't she run down to the village? There's a call-box there."

"She wanted to throw suspicion on someone, or anyone, in your house."

"I see," said Pendock again. He added, after a moment: "So you think I'm a murderer?"

"I think you constituted yourself executioner, Mr. Pendock," said Cockie with a deprecatory air.

Lady Hart was the first to break the silence. She said deliberately, sitting up very straight in her chair: "This is a terrible mistake. You've got it wrong, Inspector. You can't prove anything from all this. . . ."

"I seem to remember mentioning that point at the beginning of this little chat," said Cockie coolly. "I suggested that perhaps, if they knew him to be a murderer, his friends might put a little pressure on Mr. Pendock. . . ."

"Don't believe that *I* think you're a murderer, Pen," said Lady Hart, turning towards him, putting out her hand to him. He seemed hardly to notice it. She went on eagerly: "Couldn't it have been Trotty after all, Inspector? Never mind the snow and all that: suppose that Pippi came back here and made her call and took her scarf from the hall-stand; suppose that Trotty had followed her—perhaps had stood at the open front door and listened to what she said . . . don't you think that Trotty might have waited for her in the drive, and killed her to revenge the death of Miss Morland—or perhaps to save Fran . . . ?"

"No," said Cockrill.

She looked about her desperately, as though to find inspiration in the lovely familiar room. "But Pen—it's impossible. It's dreadful and ludicrous. Why should he have had to kill the girl? We were in the drawing-room; there was a policeman in the kitchen; he had only to raise his voice to bring us all running to his aid. Fran wasn't in danger from Pippi, once we knew what Pippi was. We could simply have overpowered her, and sent for you; you could have traced the telephone call and probably would have recognised Pippi's voice . . . we could have proved it all to you. Pen didn't *have* to kill Pippi . . . he had no *need*."

"He had no motive," said Henry quietly from his chair.

They all swung round upon him. "But Henry, if Pippi killed Grace Morland . . ."

"Pippi didn't kill Grace Morland," said Henry.

"Why do you say that?" asked Cockrill sharply.

"Your theory depends entirely on Pippi having been able to get the hat. Well, Pippi couldn't have got the hat. James and Fran came in from the orchard a few minutes after eleven, locking the back door behind them, and the hat was in the hall then. Trotty says that she went back to Pippi's room at about eleven and was talking to her there and 'listening to her tales' for more than half an hour."

Cockrill shifted his ground a little but remained unimpressed. "It isn't an important point. The fact remains that Pippi le May said over the telephone that

she was the murderer. Pendock would not have waited
to find out the rights and wrongs of it."

Pendock got suddenly to his feet. "Inspector Cockrill—you honestly think that I am responsible for this
crime?"

Cockrill was a little taken aback by so direct an at-
tack. He said, however, steadily: "I do."

"Even if you didn't, you'd be convinced that it was
at least one of us six?"

"Certainly," said Cockrill again.

Pendock shrugged his shoulders. "Then come on;
let's get on with it. Go ahead and arrest me, or whatever it is you want to do. I can't stand any more talk
and argument; I'm tired and my head's aching, and all I
want is to cease this eternal speculation and get some
peace. Let this be the end of it. Come on, do what you
want."

Fran flew to him. "Pen—Pen darling, you mustn't do
this. We know you didn't do it; don't go and say you
did . . . don't go and do something foolish. Pen! Don't
let them take you away. . . ."

He looked down at her sadly, and putting out his
hand brushed the dark curls from her forehead with
aching tenderness. "Don't cry, my little love. I don't
care; truly I don't. They can hang me by the neck until
I'm dead, and it will only be something like a release.
After all, I've got nothing to lose—have I, Fran?"

"Do you confess to this murder, Pendock?" said
Cockrill, taking Fran by the arm and pulling her aside.
· Pendock looked at him vaguely, dazed and shaking.
"Yes. Yes. Anything you like."

The two police guards advanced. Lady Hart pushed
her way between them and Pendock. "Don't you lay
hands on him! Inspector Cockrill, you're mad. Can't
you see that he's saying this to save the rest of us? He
thinks that it will never be cleared up and that suspicion and shame will rest on us all to the end of our
lives." As Cockrill caught Pendock by the arm and
shoved him towards the door, she cried desperately:
"He's innocent. You're accusing an innocent man.
He's no more a murderer than I am!"

"Very much less," said Henry evenly, and got up out
of his chair.

CHAPTER 9

They stood rooted to the floor, like a "still" from a motion picture: Pendock and Cockrill and the two guards, grouped together, half-way to the door; Lady Hart, her hands still held out towards Pendock, staring at Henry with wide eyes in a white face; Venetia sat upright in her chair, her mouth in a little round O of horrified distress; Fran was before the fireplace, petrified into stillness; James unstirring in his deep arm-chair. Henry stood in the centre, the focus of their desperate attention. He broke both stillness and silence, moving forward quietly, saying in a low, apologetic voice: "I can't let them take Pendock, Lady Hart. I'm sorry. I didn't say anything before because I thought you had—your reasons; but you can't let him take the blame. . . ."

She said wildly: "Are you suggesting that *I* killed Pippi le May?"

"*And* Grace Morland," he said, and added gently: "*Did*n't you?"

Venetia ran to him and clasped his arm. "Henry darling—no!"

"Yes, Venetia," he said wretchedly. "I'm sorry, my sweet, but—we can't let Pendock suffer, can we?"

Lady Hart had recovered herself sufficiently to come forward and sit down upon the sofa. She said, looking up at him: "When am I supposed to have killed Pippi? She was alive at eleven o'clock. At twenty-five to twelve the last train went past the summer-house. Till at least half-past eleven I was sitting in the drawing-room with you all, writing a letter to the Income Tax . . ."

"Out of sight," said Henry.

153

"Out of sight?"

"In the L of the drawing-room," said Henry again. "And so busy that you asked us not to disturb you. I'm sorry, Lady Hart."

She was silent again. After a while, in which nobody spoke, she said quietly: "All right. Tell us what you know."

"I know that Pippi was a danger to Fran," said Henry unhappily. "Not because she wanted to kill her, but because she was coming between Fran and James, because she was going to drag their names in the mud. You have a horror of notoriety and scandal, haven't you, Lady Hart? You couldn't bear to see Fran threatened, right at the beginning of her life; and she was threatened by Pippi and by Grace Morland, too. It was James and Fran that Grace Morland saw in the orchard, and it was Fran that she held in the 'hollow of her hand.' You killed her; and the next evening when Pippi was here to dinner, something must have happened to give her a clue. She might have told Pendock on her way down to the cottage, but she knew he wouldn't believe her; she decided to ring up the police, and she made an excuse to come back up to the house and do it from here. But the excuse didn't work, because Gladys told her in front of Pen that she hadn't left her glasses here; so she followed Pen back, and came into the hall while he was in the drawing-room and rang up, just as the Inspector's worked it out; and while she was standing there with the receiver in her hand, she looked up and saw you, Lady Hart, at the door of the drawing-room L, the one away from the card table. She—she was frightened. She said the first thing that came into her head: she thought you wouldn't suspect her of knowing the truth if she accused herself, and she cried out, 'This is the murderer speaking.' It would at least fetch the police; and to hurry them up, to bring them without any waste of time, she added wildly: 'Francesca's next.' Fran, or Venetia—anyone would have done: it didn't matter, if only the police would come. You would hand her over to them, and then she would be safe and could tell them what she knew."

Venetia caught his arm again. "Henry—for God's sake stop this horrible story. I won't listen to it! I hate it—I hate you. . . . If you go on with it any more, I will never speak to you again. . . ."

He looked at her sorrowfully. "I'm sorry, Venetia. I can't help it. I can't see Pendock suffer. . . ."

"Go on," said Lady Hart grimly.

"Well—Pippi's ruse didn't work, did it, Lady Hart? She would have turned away from the telephone and gone through the motions of giving herself up, pretending perhaps that she was a little bit crazy, that in a craving for sensation she had convinced herself that she was guilty of the crime; or that she was just an actress, out for publicity; but it didn't work. You got your hands round her throat; you'd done it before. And then, there she was lying dead by the telephone table, in her nasty little ocelot coat; and at any moment Pendock might come out of the other door from the drawing-room."

"Spare us the drama, Henry," said James from his arm-chair.

Henry came down to earth a little. "Well, anyway, Lady Hart just pushed the body under the table—Pendock wouldn't see it there in the hall, now that it's darkened for the black-out—or else she dragged it into the dining-room opposite. She went back to her desk and sat there writing, in the L of the drawing-room, out of sight. And when he called out 'Good-night,' she was there to answer, 'Good-night, sleep well.' "

Venetia went to her grandmother. "I don't believe one word of it, not one word."

Lady Hart took her hand in a loving grasp. "And you, Fran?"

Fran came over slowly and knelt at her feet. She looked into the old, faded blue eyes, and saw that, for the first time, Lady Hart was afraid; and she said deliberately: "I don't believe it, Gran."

"Then that's all I care about," said Lady Hart, and smiled at them gratefully.

Cockie said impatiently: "Go on with your story, Gold."

"There isn't any more of it," said Henry, looking resentfully into their hostile faces. "I say that she killed the girl and hid her, either in the hall or in the dining-room; and that after Pendock had gone up to bed she left the drawing-room again, while we were all noisily playing Vingt-et-un; she dragged the body out through the french window of the dining-room, collecting the scarf on her way; she waited until the train passed, and then she put Pippi in the summer-house and came back into the house and bolted the french window after her; and she sat down at the bureau and went on writing her letter to the Income Tax people. And the snow was still falling, covering up the prints of her high-heeled shoes. . . ."

"I will never speak to you again," said Venetia steadily.

He went and stood humbly before the little group. "I'm sorry, Venetia. I couldn't help myself." And to Lady Hart he added: "I realised this long ago. I wanted to protect you. I tried . . ."

"You tried to throw suspicion on to Trotty," said Fran roughly. "Where are all your fine professions of justice after *that*?"

He moved his head impatiently. "Trotty! Give me credit for a little common sense. It was all of *you* that suggested that Trotty had done it; and I knew well enough she could never be seriously accused. All I was trying to show was that the thing could have been done after the snow stopped falling, so as to draw attention away from all us innocent ones—and from the guilty."

Lady Hart said gravely: "But why try to protect me, if you believe me guilty?"

He looked at her with those dark, mysterious eyes. "How was I to know your reasons? Who was I to be your judge? And could I have denounced someone that Venetia loved so much . . . ?"

"You're denouncing her now," said Fran swiftly.

"Because she's letting an innocent man be accused in her place."

Lady Hart no longer looked frightened. She got to her feet and stood, holding a hand of each of her granddaughters, gathering her forces about her. "Venetia knows I'm not guilty, and so does Fran. James, do you believe this story?"

James came to with a start. "What, me, Lady Hart? Well, no. I don't think I do."

"You say that from purely sentimental reasons," said Henry angrily.

"Not at all. She was writing a letter to the Income Tax people; it was in answer to one she'd received that afternoon, so she couldn't have cooked it up before, and she showed us the finished article when she'd done. You can't write a sensible letter to the Income Tax people when you've got murder on your mind."

"This is not a laughing matter," said Henry shortly.

"I never was more serious in my life," said James.

Lady Hart looked around her with something of triumph dawning in her eyes. "And you, Pen? What do you think?"

Pendock stood silent in the doorway, in a turmoil of doubt and confusion and pain. He lifted his eyes to hers, and he remembered her white face that night as she had stood by his bed and tried to make him understand that, out in his own garden, a woman was lying murdered; remembered how she had swayed and tottered and finally fallen in a huddled heap on the floor; remembered his own frantic flight down the stairs and across the hall and over the moonlit lawns; remembered the sickening dread that had turned his legs to water as he ran—the dread that he would find Fran, his lovely one, dead in a ditch, with her beautiful head hacked off.

With her head hacked off . . .

Bunsen had called up, standing below the window, breathing heavily after his run across the grass, that there was a woman—or had he said, 'a young lady'?—lying in the garden, down by the drive. He had added: "She seems to be wearing Miss Fran's hat."

Nothing about the head.

Nothing about the head; and yet, he, Pendock, had known about the head—and only Lady Hart could have told him.

She had come into his room, and standing by his bedside she had said . . .

She had said: "Bunsen has found a girl—has seen a girl . . ." And then she had swayed and steadied herself and gone on: "There's a woman lying in the garden, down by the stream. She seems to be wearing Fran's hat. . . ."

Not a word about the head.

And suddenly he knew the truth, the real truth; and the truth was so horrible that something snapped in his brain and he lunged forward and fell, unconscious, into the arms of his guard.

Pendock was dreaming again. He dreamt that he walked down the long, familiar tunnel and that at the end, out in the sunshine, the girl was standing, her head bent down and her dark hair hiding her face. He struggled through the blackness towards her, dragging his leaden legs; she did not move, and he was shaken with the ugency of his desire to see her face. He came out of the tunnel and went up to her, and still she did not move. He put his hand beneath her chin to lift her face to the sun; and suddenly both hands were round her throat and beginning to close upon it. There was a sudden sharp pain in his leg, and at once she lifted her face, and it was Fran.

"I'm mad!" he thought. "God forgive me, I'm mad, and I'm murdering Fran. I did this to Grace Morland and I did it to Pippi le May and now I'm doing it to Fran and I can't stop myself." He had a memory of those bleeding stumps of necks, of the swing of the hatchet and the sickening scythe of the train; and above all, of the body of the girl in the wood, lying so quietly with the flashy little brooch laid neatly on her breast. "Her neck . . . her neck . . . I couldn't get it out of my mind. The thought of it, the sight of it, the terrible smell of the blood . . ."

There was a swirling blackness about him and then the sunlight again, and he had Fran's throat in his hands and was forcing her head back, squeezing her throat and forcing her head back; he knew he would break her neck. "I must stop," he thought. "This is Fran—Fran whom I love; I don't want to hurt her—it's Fran." But his hands would not obey. Again there was a sharp, sweet, sickly pain in his leg, and the wave of sanity returned.

Grace Morland. Lying in the ditch, made horrible and disgusting by the bright little hat perched on her lolling head. "She shouldn't have sneered at Fran; she came running up to the house and said she had seen Fran kissing James in the orchard; she said filthy things about her, obscene and filthy things. . . . I killed her, I strangled her and hacked off her ugly head. She shouldn't have sneered at Fran. . . ."

The darkness descended upon him again, great waves of horror and helplessness and despair. He got a sort of backward glimpse of Pippi as he had come upon her at the telephone in the hall; of her staring eyes and suddenly faltering voice, of the feel of his hands about her throat, squeezing, squeezing, squeezing . . . as he was doing to Fran. But this was Fran, not Pippi: this was Fran. Something behind him in the tunnel was dragging at his legs.

"I'm going to kill her," he thought. "I love her, but I'm going to kill her. I'm mad, I can't stop myself." And through the chaos of his mind a thought, straight from the great, good heart, beat like a gong. "I ought to be destroyed. I'm dangerous. I ought to be dead."

Hands were dragging at him. A voice cried: "Shoot! Why don't you shoot?" A voice said, agonised: "I daren't; I should hit the girl." Fran had a revolver, somebody had given her a revolver; voices were crying: "We can't get him off you. Shoot! Press it against his body and shoot! SHOOT!"

He tore the revolver out of her grasp and pointed it round him blindly, not knowing what he did. He held

Fran braced against his body; she was calling out to him, pleading with him: "Pen, let me go! Pen, don't you know me? It's Fran. Pen, let me go!"

He must get to her throat again. His fingers began to curl for the feel of it, for the sweet, warm feel of her throat, Fran's throat, who would never be his. I ought to be dead. I ought to be destroyed. I'm mad, I'm dangerous, and this is Fran. I ought to be dead.

Good and Evil: heart and mind wrestled together in the few black seconds that lasted a hundred years. I, Pendock, I'm mad. I'm dangerous. I'm nothing better than a mad dog; I ought to be destroyed. Why don't they kill me, why don't they save her from me? And then, triumphant, ringing like a clarion through the wreckage of the splendid brain: "I must save Fran. I must save her. I must save her from myself!"

He dragged his hands from her throat and, hugging the revolver to him, pulled the trigger.

"I couldn't hold him, sir," said Johnson to Cockrill in a frightened and penitent voice. "I caught him as he fell, but I thought it was just a faint. I wasn't prepared for him to struggle, and he tore himself away from me and went for the girl. If that dog hadn't attacked him, sir—but each time it went for his legs, he seemed to slacken his hold on her throat a bit; I do believe it saved her life, sir. She couldn't have held out otherwise. . . ."

Fran was on the floor beside Pendock's body, holding her aching throat. "Oh, he's dead, he's dead. Pen darling—Pen, I'm so sorry. He couldn't help it; he didn't know what he was doing. He must have been mad all the time; poor Pen. Oh, Granny, he was mad!"

"Yes, darling," said Lady Hart, and took her by the arm and pulled her to her feet. "Come away now; you can't do Pen any good. He's dead, and it's better that way: isn't it, darling? Isn't it better that way?"

"He killed himself because he couldn't save me any other way," cried Fran, and leant her head against James's breast and sobbed. "Oh, James, I'm so frightened, and it's all so dreadful and my throat aches most terribly! Pen! Pen! Who could have believed that he was mad? Dear Pen . . . he loved me and he was so sweet. . . ."

"Take her somewhere else," said Cockie to James. He bent down and closed the eyelids over the beautiful blue-green eyes. "God rest his soul! Who could have known he was mad?"

"We ought to have recognised the signs," said Lady Hart sadly, sitting down in a chair and covering her face with her hands. "He never knew, of course. But he got these headaches . . . And yet—there's nothing in the family."

"His mother died young," said Cockrill thoughtfully, "and she died abroad. We never knew quite what happened."

"But he always seemed such a normal, steady person: what could have suddenly turned his brain like that?"

"I wonder if it was the death of that girl in the wood," said Venetia, looking up swiftly. "He was so terribly upset by it; perhaps it shook him worse than we realised. We mentioned it here, in the drawing-room, that afternoon when Grace Morland came to tea—don't you remember, Granny? He went so white, and he shuddered all over, and later in the evening he said he had a headache. He had one the night Pippi died, too: I remember thinking how white he looked, but I supposed he hadn't got over the fright when Fran disappeared. You do think he—forgot all about it? He never knew what he'd done?"

"Oh, I'm sure he didn't: if he'd guessed for a moment that he was a danger to other people, he'd have given himself up. In certain types there's a sort of automatism, at least I think I'm right in saying so: they act abnormally, and don't know what they're doing at all; then there's a period while they act perfectly naturally, but still automatically, and when they come to, they just think they've been asleep; and of course poor Pen believed he'd been in bed all night."

They stood round, staring with pitiful eyes as two constables lifted the body and carried it up-stairs. Henry said diffidently: "Forgive me, Lady Hart."

She could not smile, but she put out her hand to him and said, as she had said earlier in the evening: "You did quite right, Henry; you were only doing what seemed right"; and to Venetia, sitting shivering alone on the sofa, she added gently: "He protected me while he thought nobody else would suffer through it, Venetia; he said it was not for him to judge me. He did quite right to speak, when he thought the wrong person was being accused. If *I* can understand that, you must," and watched them as he humbly took Venetia's hand and kept it in his own.

Cockie had steadied his shaking fingers sufficiently to roll himself a cigarette. He said abruptly: "What do you think happened? Why Grace Morland?"

"It was because of Fran, I suppose," said Lady Hart. "He was a little excited already that afternoon; then Miss Morland abused her on the way down to the cottage. But how did he get her out into the garden that night?"

"Don't you think she may have come of her own accord?" suggested Henry. "She looked out of her bedroom window and saw Fran kissing James in the orchard; and in her hate and jealousy she slipped out of the cottage while Trotty was talking in Pippi's room, and came up to the house; perhaps she threw stones at Pendock's window like Bunsen did, and she poured out to Pendock some filthy story about Fran. . . ."

"He was very much in love with Fran," said Cockie, looking at the tip of his cigarette.

"Yes, he was. Too much in love with her. She wasn't—big enough for it," said Lady Hart frankly. "I don't mean to say that Fran's shallow, because I don't think she is; but she's young and gay and light-hearted and often silly; she's not cut out for the *grande passion,* and Pen just loved her too much." She added thoughtfully: "I was glad to see how, in her bad moment, she turned to James."

"James loves her too," said Venetia, with a soft little sigh, and she turned upon Henry adoring eyes, and was his slave again.

Henry still held tightly to her hand, but he did not even notice that she had spoken. He said, with a return to his old bouncing eagerness: "So Pippi did come up to the house that night and telephone! She must have noticed something in Pendock's manner as they went down to the Cottage; you remember how headachy and nervy he was. . . ."

Lady Hart looked up suddenly: "Do you know what it was . . . he said to Pippi as they went through the hall that . . . I forget quite what, but something to the effect that it had been terrible running out into the garden, expecting to find Fran with her head cut off—he said it several times to all of us, and none of us ever spotted that of course he couldn't have known that Grace Morland had been decapitated, unless he had done it himself. I suppose it was a sort of half-memory. . . . But Pippi was such a smart, clever little creature; *she* realised. And brave too, if you think what she did then . . . she came right back to this house to try and warn us: I do believe that's what she did! She made an excuse about the glasses; but when that failed she just simply followed him back and came into the hall. She heard him talking to us in the drawing-room . . ."

"And I'll tell you what," said Henry excitedly, as the pieces of the puzzle began at last to fall into place. "She heard Fran ask him to stay and play Vingt-et-un. Don't you remember, Venetia, that you heard something out in the hall, just about the same time . . . you thought it must have been Aziz. Pippi must have decided that Pen would be harmlessly playing cards with us for a good time to come, so she decided to ring up the police . . . and Pendock found her at it and silenced her. All that part that I worked out for—Lady Hart—was right. Pippi saw that he had heard her asking for Cockrill: she lost her head and said frantically that she was the murderess, and tried to hurry them up by adding that Fran was 'next'; he waited till she had finished and then he killed her. He cut the lines of the telephone. . . ."

"They get a sort of heightened—cunning," said Lady Hart, shuddering away from the ugly word.

"And then he took her down to the railway line, collecting the scarf as he went. . . ."

"No. He came back for the scarf," said Cockrill. "He always insisted that the murderer 'came back to the house for the scarf.' Another half-memory."

They fell into a reverie again; Lady Hart said sadly: "Sometimes there are dreams—a recurrent dream, not necessarily anything bad or terrible, but always the same one. I wonder if Pen had a dream. . . ."

The two constables had carried Pendock's body upstairs and laid it on his own bed. The shot had gone through the heart, and they thrust a towel between his hand and his breast to dry up the pool of blood. A photograph fell out of his breast pocket and on to the floor.

"It's Fran," said Cockie, and wiped off the blood and put it back gently into the lifeless hand.

CHAPTER 10

An older and quieter Fran stood, six months later, in her bridal dress, having her veil arranged. Aziz barked ecstatically round her feet. "He knows we don't often get married," said Venetia, seizing him in her arms and kissing his soft brown face.

"Venetia darling, *don't* let him lick you!"

"Oh, Granny, it can't possibly do any harm, except to my war-paint. Fran darling, honestly, you look divine."

"You don't look so bad yourself," said Fran, smiling at her sister's reflection beside her in the glass. "Henry, what are you doing here? Why aren't you in the church, looking after James?"

"James is in the front pew, darling, completely oblivious to his surroundings, reading the 'Sonnets to a Dark Lady,' disguised as Hymns A. and M. I just slipped over to wish you . . . well, you know all that I can possibly wish you, Fran. I hope James will always love you as truly and deeply as I love Venetia; and if you give him even a part of what Venetia has given me . . ."

"*Don't* get all Jewish and sentimental, darling, or I shall start howling. Aziz, my heavenly one, come and kiss your mother before she gets her face on."

"Fran, don't let him lick your face. . . ."

The sun shone, the fortifying champagne whispered in their shallow glasses, Fran's flowers were perfect, Venetia had split her glove, Lady Hart was convinced that her grey frock made her look like an elephant. "But, darling, some elephants are *sweet*. . . ."

They all hung out of the window, waving to the guests going into the church next door. "There's that awful Miss Whatsaname—Granny, you are a traitor, I *told* you not to ask her! There's Mrs. Pountney, what a nice hat!—and, look, there's Aunt Aggie, and she's got her handkerchief out all ready to weep when I say, 'I will.' Is it 'I will' that I say?"

"If you can bring yourself to be so obliging for once," said Venetia. She waved violently to a black beetle on the pavement outside the church. "It's Cockie! Fancy him coming all the way up from Torrington; bless his heart!"

"So it is," said Francesca. She waved her bouquet frantically out of the window. "Cockie! Oi, Cockie! this is me, Fran, all dressed up like a Christmas tree. I'm getting married to-day."

Cockie waved back at them and replaced his hat at its Napoleonic angle upon his head. "Thank goodness he can't keep it on in church," said Lady Hart, leaning out of the other window, no less excited than they. "Isn't that Trotty? He must have brought her up in his car."

"And Bunsen; dear old Bunsen! Hallo, Bunsen, how very grand you look!"

"Miss Fran," cried Bunsen, shocked to his respectable core. "You shouldn't be showing yourself. I beg your pardon, my lady, but the bride shouldn't be seen, you know. . . ."

Fran drew in her head and readjusted her veil. "I wish they hadn't come; and yet I don't." She dabbed at her face with a powder puff, leaning forward and peering into the mirror. "Well, come on; what about it? Shouldn't we start?"

The bridesmaids were huddled in a giggling group at the foot of the stairs. Lady Hart pulled a sash straight, adjured two young flappers to hold their stomachs in, and shaking her head anxiously over the vision of a charming grey elephant that met her from a passing mirror, swept out of the hotel and into the church next door. The bridesmaids formed themselves into something like a procession and an elderly uncle offered Fran his arm. Venetia went ahead of them, Aziz clasped to her bosom.

A verger halted her at the big door of the church: "Pardon me, Miss, but not the little dog."

The ancient struggle began all over again. "He'll be perfectly quiet and no one will notice him. Do let me take him inside; he does want to see her married."

"Is this the bride's dog, Miss?"

"He is now," said Venetia. She explained to him earnestly: "I've given her my half for a wedding present. He used to belong to us both, but—well, once, he sort of helped to save her life. . . ."

Fran and the elderly uncle arrived in the porch. "Won't they let Aziz come in?"

"I'm afraid he must stay outside, Miss. I'll hold him here, if you like."

Venetia drew her sister a little aside. "Let the man hold him; he won't be outside for long!" She added softly: "I told him that Aziz saved your life, and it made me think—while we're so happy, Fran, I think—just for a minute—we should remember Pen."

"It was Pen that saved my life," said Fran, standing there in her white dress at the door of the beautiful old church. "It wasn't Aziz; nobody saved my life but Pen himself. It was right of you to remind me, darling, but I hadn't forgotten. He gave his life to save mine—dear Pen!" They smiled at each other and there were tears in their eyes.

Fran went up to the altar to meet James; and outside the church Aziz began to howl.

NERO WOLFE STEPS OUT

Every Wolfe Watcher knows that the world's largest detective wouldn't dream of leaving the brownstone on 35th street, with Fritz's three star meals, his beloved orchids and the only chair that actually suits him. But when an ultra-conservative college professor winds up dead and Archie winds up in jail, Wolfe is forced to brave the wilds of upstate New York to find a murderer.

THE BLOODIED IVY
by Robert Goldsborough
A Bantam Hardcover
05281 $15.95

and don't miss these other Nero Wolfe mysteries by Robert Goldsborough:

☐ 27024 **DEATH ON DEADLINE** $3.95
            —FINALLY IN PAPERBACK!
☐ 26120 **MURDER IN E MINOR** $3.50

"A Smashing Success"—*Chicago Sun–Times*

And Bantam still offers you a whole series of Nero Wolfe mysteries by his creator, Rex Stout

☐ 24730   **DEATH OF A DUDE** $2.95
☐ 24918   **FER-DE-LANCE** $2.95
☐ 25172   **GAMBIT** $2.95
☐ 25425   **DEATH TIMES THREE** $2.95
☐ 25254   **FINAL DEDUCTION** $2.95

Look for them at your bookstore or use the coupon below: